Operation Cinderella

A Suddenly Cinderella Novel

Hope Tarr

Entangled Publishing, LLC
2614 South Timberline Road
Suite 109
Fort Collins, CO 80525
Visit our website at www.entangledpublishing.com.

Edited by Stacy Abrams
Cover design by Libby Murphy

ISBN   978-1-62266-849-6

Manufactured in the United States of America

First Edition October 2012

The author acknowledges the copyrighted or trademarked status and trademark owners of the following wordmarks mentioned in this work of fiction: Pepto-Bismol, Newsweek, Boston speakers, Jimmy Choo, iPhone, iPod, Dumpster, BlackBerry, Jell-O, Extra Strength Tylenol, Bergdorf's, Playboy, Oscar, Barbacide, The Bird Cage, Disney, Saks Fifth Avenue, Talbots, Burberry, Barbie, Guinness, Harp, Barbour, Manolo Blahnik, North by Northwest, American Eagle Outfitters, Ducoti, Coke, Ann Taylor, Victoria's Secret, Lawrence of Arabia, Bonanza, Wikipedia, Express, Ford Explorer, Amtrak, Starbucks, Häagen-Dazs, Coors, Brooks Brothers, La Perla, Post-it, Armani, Dior, Boone's Farm, Pizza Hut, Facebook, Twitter, Pinterest, Brylcreem.

To my two fairy godmothers, otherwise known as agents, Lori Perkins and Louise Fury. Thanks for making me believe again...

Once upon a time in a faraway land, a forest of steel and concrete known as Manhattan…

Prologue

"Keep your jock strap on, I'm coming."

Macie Graham stepped out of the shower to her apartment buzzer blaring. Fuck, that was fast. She'd been ordering from All Thai'd Up for two years now, at first because the edgy whimsy of the name appealed to her and later because they screwed up her standard order of Panang Curry with a side of sticky rice fewer times than the average St. Mark's take-out dive. Bonus: the restaurant was only a few blocks from her apartment. Still, this was the first time one of their bicycle delivery guys had made it to her building in sub-fifteen minutes. Dude must be a regular Lance Armstrong. Impressive.

The buzzer let out another ear-splitting screech. Okay, this was getting annoying. Grabbing her robe off the hook, she called out from the steam-filled bathroom, "Chill already, I said I'm coming." A stupid thing to do, literally talking to the walls, and yet considering all the stupid to bad things she'd done in the past month and a half, talking to herself didn't begin to make the list.

She wrapped a towel around her streaming wet hair and raced through the living room, emptied of possessions except for her inflatable mattress, single suitcase, and her cat Stevie's feeding bowls. Aside from the few boxes in her bedroom, everything else was in storage—in limbo like the rest of her life.

Reaching the door to her apartment—well, hers until tomorrow—she punched the intercom button. "Sorry, I was in the—"

"MJ…Macie, or whatever the hell you're calling yourself these days, I know you're in there. Buzz me up—*now!*" Ross's voice, armed with an angry edge, rose above the crackling.

Oh shit, oh shit, oh shit…

Whipping away from the intercom, Macie pressed her damp back against the double-bolt, emotions reeling between shock, elation, and a primal fear. Ross. What was he doing here? How had he found her? And now that he had, how could she convince him to go away?

"Macie, it's no use pretending. I talked to Francesca. She told me everything."

At the mention of Ross's ex-wife, every pore in Macie's body seemed to open, soaking her terry cloth robe. She swallowed deeply, sucking down air like a college freshman quaffing beer at a kegger.

So this is what a panic attack feels like. I always wondered. Maybe I'll do a story on it someday. Someday—assuming I survive.

She closed her eyes and focused on her breathing. Had she really gone from features editor of *On Top Magazine*, one of the hottest, hippest women's magazines to come on the scene since *Jane*, to hunted fugitive in six short weeks?

"Macie, I know you're in there."

Ross's voice, angry sounding but weary, too, dragged her back to the madness of the moment. It was time to pull up her Big Girl pants and face the so-called music…which hopefully wouldn't involve either police sirens or angel harps.

"Buzz me in and hear me out. You owe me that much."

Swallowing hard, Macie opened her eyes and turned back around. He was right. She owed him that much. That much and so much more.

She reached out a trembling hand and punched in the security code.

Chapter One

OFFICES OF ON TOP MAGAZINE, MIDTOWN MANHATTAN
SEPTEMBER, SIX WEEKS EARLIER

"Graham, I want your ass in my office in ten minutes. Ten minutes—got it?" Over the crackle of intercom static, Starr's pissed voice reverberated off the framed magazine cover blow-ups blanketing the walls of Macie's office.

Macie opened her mouth to answer, "Sure thing," just as the line clicked dead. Her managing editor had just hung up on her. Could a pink slip be far behind?

She jerked open a desk drawer and searched inside for something to kill the headache hammering her skull, the double whammy of too many dirty martinis in celebration of Labor Day the night before and being blindsided that morning by her latest ballsy editorial decision blowing up in her face. No aspirin, just her luck—but there was a travel-size bottle of Pepto-Bismol. Loosening the child safety cap almost cost a sculpted nail, but once she had it off, she brought the bottle to her lips and knocked back a soothing bubblegum pink swallow.

Setting the antacid aside, she faced her computer screen, loathing bubbling up like bile. "You...asshole!"

The asshole, conservative media pundit Ross Mannon, smiled back at her from the webcast she'd paused in mid-play. With his cropped dark blond hair, chiseled features, and cerulean blue eyes, it didn't take much imagination to recognize why the female *Newsweek* reporter had dubbed him the Robert Redford of the Right.

The Texas sociologist had made national headlines the year before by publicizing his research study showing a strong positive correlation between the hours American teens spent online and their likelihood to engage in a laundry list of high-risk behaviors, including unprotected intercourse. The conservative media had latched onto the study's findings like a starved leech let loose inside a Red Cross blood bank. Within a week, "Dr. Ross" was making guest appearances on national news talk shows, decrying the country's "culture of part-time parenting couched in denial and politically correct double speak." Six months ago, he'd landed his own daily weekday radio program broadcast from the nation's capital. Currently, three hundred radio stations around the country had picked up "The Ross Mannon Hour" as part of their regular programming, and the show's website pulled in around 100,000 visits per day.

Until now, Macie had left Mannon alone. *On Top* might run some pretty candid — okay, in-your-face — copy, but taking on the latest conservative media messiah qualified as just plain stupid.

It was Mannon who'd put the kibosh on their peaceful coexistence. He'd gotten his hands on a copy of *On Top*'s current issue, spotted Macie's feature article on the growing number of parents opting to prevent unwanted pregnancies by putting their teenage daughters on birth control *before* they had sex—"Forget the Fairy Tale. Teen Sex is Fact, Not Fiction"—and made the magazine the target of that morning's "Ross's Rant." He'd ended by giving out *On Top*'s website, mailing address, *and* toll-free phone number, urging his listeners to make their voices heard. Within minutes the magazine's overloaded server had crashed and the switchboard had lit up like a billboard in Times Square.

Along with the phone calls, which had ranged from hostile to deranged, there'd been e-mails to the corporate Powers That Be denouncing Macie's article as trash. Macie hadn't really worried much about that. *On Top*'s readership and Ross Mannon's radio audience were planets apart, a separate species of entertainment news consumer. But when a major advertising account, Beauté, a manufacturer of high-end hair care products targeting the "tween" to teen market, pulled the ad spread they ran in every issue, citing the morals clause in their contract and concerns over branding and corporate image, well, that was another story.

She clicked her mouse to maximize the clip. Mannon's blond head and broad shoulders filled her screen, and for a crazy few seconds she forgot why she was supposed to hate him. More than his looks, though, there was something in his eyes that brought to mind long-forgotten fairy tale fantasies about knights in shining armor, princes capable of bringing you back to life with a single, petal-soft kiss, and True Love, forever-after love, the kind of Big Love that outlasted a single sexy weekend or hot hook-up night—only, of course, it didn't really exist.

All that perfection had to be a smokescreen, a front. Picture-perfect types like Mannon invariably had a less than storybook behind-the-scenes. He was altogether too good-looking, too *hot* to be living the squeaky-clean life of a contemporary Prince Charming. His website bio, pared down to a smattering of innocuous factoids, stood out as a big friggin' red flag. Born and raised in Paris, Texas. A football scholarship to the University of North Texas, where he'd stayed on to earn a PhD. One daughter, Samantha, but no mention of a wife, which almost certainly meant he was divorced. *Hypocrite!* Do a little digging and the frog hanging out inside the pretty boy prince would leap to the surface. Just give her the chance, the access, and she could blow Mannon's cover—she *knew* it.

It was all about the access.

She pulled at the ends of her waist-length hair, now straightened and colored jet black, and clicked on the pause button to pick up where she'd left off viewing the video.

Mannon's deep-timbered Texas drawl blared from her Boston speakers. "Folks, I don't usually bring up personal stuff on the air, but I'm gonna go ahead and make an exception. Looks like my fifteen-year-old daughter, Samantha, is going to be living with me twenty-four-seven for the foreseeable future, and the plain truth is I'm not much of a cook or a housekeeper…"

The plain truth. Ha! I'll bet you wouldn't recognize the truth if it bit you on your uptight ass.

"But what my Sam needs more than any of those things, even more than someone to chauffeur her around—and believe me, that kid's schedule is packed tighter than the president's—is a role model, a lady who models the kind of core values we talk about on this show."

Macie fought the urge to gag. Poor kid. Sight unseen, she felt an affinity with Mannon's daughter, whose situation struck her as eerily similar to her own childhood. It hadn't been easy growing up as a precocious free-spirit. But when you were born to people—trolls—whose idea of parenting meant crushing independent thought at every turn, holding onto your self-worth, not to mention your sanity, was a constant struggle.

"Last Sunday," Mannon continued, "I ran an ad in the *Washington Times* online. 'Wanted: woman with old-fashioned values to serve as live-in housekeeper, child care provider, and female role model for precocious fifteen-year-old girl. Salary and benefits negotiable; values firm.' You'd think ad copy like that would make it pretty clear what type of person I'm looking for, and yet would you believe I must have interviewed a dozen applicants this past week, and the last one showed up with green hair and a nose ring?"

Macie slid a hand over her stomach, feeling the small gold belly button hoop below her cropped body-hugging black angora sweater, and listened on.

"Okay, that's enough about my domestic issues. This show is first and foremost about *you*. If any of you listening out there have a topic you'd like us to address in a future Ross's Rant, shoot me an e-mail and put 'Rant' in the subject header. Again, that's r-o-s-s at r-o-s-s-m-a-n-n-o-n dot com."

Macie stared at the screen, feeling as if steam must be jetting out of her ears. Pretty clever—make that *devious*—getting his listeners to come up with the content for his upcoming broadcasts. Slacker!

She had her middle finger pointed to the ceiling when it hit her. Holy shit, it really was all about the access. Mannon had just handed her the proverbial keys to the kingdom.

Adrenaline pumping, she signed off from the *On Top* local area network and logged on to her personal account. Typing Mannon's e-mail address into the Send box took balls, but still, it was the easy part. Crafting a message he would buy was trickier. Sticking to the K.I.S.S. rule, Keep It Simple, Stupid, she pounded out a few simple sentences aimed at balancing the requisite background information with just enough bait. She read it over one last time, clicked Send, and darted a look at the chrome-encased wall clock. 4:28. *Two minutes to spare—damn, I'm good.*

She shoved her feet into her Jimmy Choo platform sling-backs, grabbed her iPhone, and shot up from the desk. Stepping out into the neon-lit hallway, she pulled the office door closed behind her. Fairy tales were for kids. Exposing a fake prince for his true frog self—real grownup life didn't pack more magical mojo than that.

• • •

WATERGATE TOWERS, NORTHWEST WASHINGTON DC

"Sam, I'm home." Ross Mannon stepped inside the condo foyer and pulled the door closed behind him. He wasn't ordinarily home by five p.m., but then this had been a *special* day.

No answer came, not that he'd really expected one, but the backpack dumped by the door told him that Samantha was home. Still, the place was so quiet an ice cube cracking would have sounded like a siren. Ice wasn't far from the truth, either. His daughter was dishing out the classic cold shoulder treatment—and he was definitely being served.

He dropped his keys on the marble-top foyer table and headed down the beige-carpeted hallway to her bedroom, the scene of his latest parental crime cop bust. Her door was closed—no big surprise there. His fourth knuckle-bruising knock finally brought her to answer it.

She opened it a crack, just enough for him to make out one watery eye and a sliver of pink-rimmed nose. Shit, she'd been crying. *Call me Father of the Year—not!* "What do you want now?"

Taking a breath, he reminded himself he was the adult in

this situation. "You and I have some talking to do."

The door widened another notch, revealing a ribbon of stiffened upper lip and a sliver of white wire from her iPod headphones. "I don't feel like it."

"Feel like it or not, we're going to settle this thing once and for all. Be in my study in five minutes or you're grounded for the week."

She backed up and drew the door closed on what skirted a slam.

So much for starting fresh.

Feeling as exhausted as if he'd just butted heads with Rita Mae Brown, Ross turned and headed down the hall to his study, his sanctuary in an apartment that otherwise felt too super-sized, too sleekly trendy, and entirely too beige to ever really suit him. That's what came of hiring an interior designer, he supposed. At least he'd stuck to his guns and kept her out of his study. The room's mission-style furnishings, terra cotta colors, and Navaho woven rug were purely him...as were his books, leather-bound editions of American literary classics from Nathaniel Hawthorne to Mark Twain to Arthur Miller, all of which he'd had shipped from his ranch back in Texas. After six months in the city, the study still smelled slightly of...home.

A stab of homesickness struck. Determined to ignore it, he stepped behind the desk, took out his computer, and hit the power button. Logging on and scrolling through his e-mail inbox, he promised himself that unlike the magazine mishap that morning, which he'd bungled badly, he wouldn't lose his head. If the kid was angry, then let her be angry. Any emotion, even rage, was preferable to the smoldering silence she dished out most days.

A huff drew his gaze to the door. Sam stood on the threshold, one bare foot braced out in the hallway as though she was already planning her exit strategy, her escape.

In a single glance, he took in her mousse-spiked hair, belly-baring T-shirt, and low-rise jeans and felt his parental self-esteem sinking like the *Titanic*. His baby girl, where had she gone, and who was this sullen, slouching stranger? Heavy black liner rimmed angry blue eyes, taking him back to the month before when she'd shown up in the lobby of his Watergate condominium post midnight, a backpack slung over one bony shoulder and rivulets of mascara running like muddy rivers down her cheeks.

"I'm not going back to Mom's, and you can't make me," were the first words out of her mouth, her chin—shaped just like her mother's—pointed due north.

He hadn't been sure what to do first: shake the shit out of her for talking to him like that or hug her because she was, after all, safe and not lying dead in a Dumpster. He'd opted for the hug, squared things with the doorman, and then hurried her upstairs to his apartment. As soon as he'd closed the door behind them, her tough-girl exterior crumbled like a cookie.

"Oh, Daddy…" she cried in that little girl voice he remembered so well, the voice that not only pulled on his heartstrings but threatened to snap them clean through.

And that's when he'd known Sam wasn't just acting out. For her to run away, something had gone wrong, *very* wrong, back in New York.

Just when he sensed she was on the brink of opening up to him, his BlackBerry belted out the first few bars to Madonna's "Material Girl," the ringtone he'd assigned to his ex-wife, Francesca.

Sam had closed up like a clam. Sobbing, she made a beeline for his spare bedroom, the one earmarked for her when she came to stay.

The opportunity lost, Ross picked up the call. "Frannie,

listen up. Sam's here. She's safe." He spent the next thirty minutes calming her down while trying to figure out what had gone so terribly wrong

Only, Frannie was clueless, too, which scared the crap out of him. Until now, his ex had always been the cool parent, the confidante, the cross between a best friend and a big sister. If she was in the dark, then whatever had gone wrong with Sam wasn't small. It was major. Learning that she'd apparently shoplifted a bullshit charm bracelet a few weeks before had stunned him to his core.

"How the hell did that happen?" he'd demanded. "And why am I just hearing about it now?"

"Don't interrogate me, Ross," Frannie snapped, her British sangfroid on the cusp of a major meltdown. "I know you think I'm a bloody poor parent but—"

"That's not true."

Frannie was no Mrs. Cleaver, that was for damned sure, but she loved Sam with all her heart. He might disapprove of her travel schedule and crazy work hours—he *did* disapprove— but she was a good mom. And a kid, a girl especially, needed her mother, which was why he hadn't fought for shared custody, settling instead for seeing Sam during summers and every other holiday.

He drew a deep breath and dropped his voice. "Look, whatever went wrong for Samantha went down in New York, and it's obvious she sees DC and my apartment as her haven—for now, anyway. Let me get her calmed down, enroll her in school here, and see what happens. Just before you called, she was close to confiding in me. I could *feel* it."

That last statement had won Francesca over. In the end, they'd agreed he would keep Sam with him, but only until the winter break. In the meantime, he had his work cut out for him. He hadn't been a full-time parent for years. Hell, he hadn't been much of a part-time one, either. Still, he'd always thought his relationship with his daughter was pretty solid. Staring at her now, he admitted he'd been kidding himself. Just how well did he really know her? What was she into? Who were her friends? What were her plans for the future, her dreams? Did she even have any? More than the all-black clothing and the tongue stud, it was the dull, dead look in her eyes that had him worrying. Just last summer she'd seemed so bright-eyed, so…happy.

"Why are you looking at me all weird like that?" Sam's voice snapped him back to the present. "If you have some big-deal thing to say to me, then say it."

"Okay, I will." He cleared his throat, steeling himself to deal with the proverbial elephant in the room: the confiscated magazine. Not yet able to go there, he started out with, "First off, I want you to know I'm working on getting someone to help us out around here. You know, keep house and cook and drive you back and forth to school and anywhere else you need to go so you won't be stuck here when I'm held up at the studio." *Someone to watch over you when I can't. Someone, a woman, to help me figure out what the hell's going on with you before it's too late.*

Her eyes narrowed. "Isn't that what Mrs. Alvarez does?"

"Well, sort of. But Mrs. A doesn't drive." Nor was she young or cool enough for Sam to consider her as anything but an authority figure.

She snapped out of her slouch. "So you fired her!"

Ross stiffened. Why was she so hell-bent on seeing him as some kind of ogre?

Reaching for what was left of his patience, he said, "I did not. Mrs. A asked for a leave of absence to help out with her new grandbaby. I told her she can come back whenever she's ready."

It was the truth, though judging from Sam's face, she wasn't buying it. Lower lip dropping, she raked a hand through her hair, the nails painted black and bitten to the quick.

"Seeing as we have an extra bedroom nobody's using, I figured it would be easier if we had someone stay here instead of commuting," he added.

Whatever he'd said, it set her off like a firecracker on the Fourth of July. "You're hiring a live-in!" she shouted, eyes blazing. "Is *she* going to search my room, too?"

Finally, the elephant in the room wasn't only acknowledged but paraded around like a prize pony. "Honey, I wasn't searching your room. When you didn't answer my knock this morning, I thought you'd overslept. I didn't want you to be late for school."

Late for school, my ass. He'd been scared shitless she might have done something to hurt herself. Maybe he was just being paranoid, but she'd been acting so depressed and secretive, he hardly knew what to expect. Hearing the shower running in her bathroom, he'd heaved a sigh of relief. She was running late, end of story. He'd turned to go when the *On Top Magazine* lying open on the nightstand snagged his attention. The article title, "Forget the Fairy Tale: Teen Sex is Fact, Not Fiction" caught his eye, but it was the subtitle that had him seeing red. "Why smart parenting means prepping your daughter with condoms, the Pill..."

Staring at those big bold block letters, Ross had felt like he'd been belted with a thunderbolt from the sky and a sucker punch to the gut all rolled into one terrifying freeze-frame moment. Time seemed to stop. His breathing seemed to stop. Everything seemed to stop, everything except for the fear. Was Sam thinking about having sex or was she already having it? And if she was having it, was she having it with or without protection? Did protection mean condoms or the Pill, both, or neither? If the answer to any of those questions was yes, then clearly he was doing the asking way late, maybe even... too late? Too late—and his baby was just fifteen!

No previous ah-ha moment had ever hit him so hard or hurt so much. Somehow he'd become one of *those* parents— the parents he railed about on his radio show—the ones so selfishly wrapped up in their own lives they didn't have a clue where or *who* their kid was. Now he was one of them, a lost tribe awash in denial. While he'd been the parental equivalent of Rip Van Winkle, his Sam was being poisoned with toxic cultural messages. The rage ripping through him had required an outlet and there'd been just one place for it to go. He'd picked up the magazine, screwed it into a tight cylinder, and shoved it beneath his arm.

"When I saw that"—*rag, piece of trash*—"publication, I..."—*overreacted? Okay, flipped out*—"felt concerned. That's not the kind of material you should be exposed to at your age." *Or ever*, he wanted to add, but since he couldn't protect her indefinitely, he could at least exercise the three years of parental rights he had left under the law.

She folded her arms across her chest like body armor, an age-old symbol of defiance. "That's my decision."

He glanced down at her latest "decision," a gold naval ring, and felt another piece of his soul chip away. "No, honey, I'm afraid it's not. As long as you're under eighteen, your mom and I are responsible for you."

She let out a sharp laugh, the cynicism slashing at his heart. "Funny, Mom never censored my reading. Or my Internet access," she added, referencing the parental controls he'd activated within hours of her appearance.

Maybe she should have, he thought, but loyalty and something else, something deeper, held him back from saying so. Frannie had shouldered the main responsibility for raising

Sam for a decade. Dissing her decidedly more permissive parenting style when she wasn't present to defend herself wouldn't be fair to her or good for Sam.

Instead he said, "As long as you're living under my roof, you'll abide by my rules." Good Lord, he'd gone from old to positively Paleolithic.

She stared back at him, cheeks red and eyes defiant. "Maybe I won't be 'under your roof' for much longer."

Her lower lip quivered, reminding him of when she'd been little and a skinned knee or broken doll had brought her running to him to make it all better. Back then he'd been her knight in shining armor, her hero to the rescue. If only he could figure out a way to rescue her now.

"Look, Sam, if something's...*wrong*...there's nothing you could ever do to make me or your mom stop loving you. Come here, baby." He stood and stretched his arms out into the empty space between them, willing her to meet him, if only halfway.

"Not this time, Daddy." Eyes on the verge of overflowing, she turned and ran, bare feet pummeling down the hallway.

Absorbing each retreating thud like a gut punch, he dropped his arms to his sides. The familiar sound of her door slamming sent him folding into the leather desk chair. *Good going, Mannon. Now she* really *hates you.*

Scouring a hand over his forehead, he reached into his desk drawer and brought out the magazine. *On Top.* He flipped through, stopping at the cover story. He'd read it several times now, but like a kid picking at a scab, he couldn't resist another look. Laced with interview quotes, slanted statistics, and colorful sidebar anecdotes, it wasn't badly written even if its message was crap. *Forget the Fairy Tale...* He shook his head, thinking of another word beginning with *F* and swearing it beneath his breath.

As if it wasn't confusing enough being a teenager, the media had to put out the message that there was no such thing as Mr. Right, let alone Prince Charming. Apparently the best a young woman could hope for was Mr. Right Now, and parents could expect their daughters to go through several Mr. Right Nows before the age of twenty-one. *Jesus H. Christ!* Teens, both boys and girls, needed to understand that promiscuity brought consequences, *serious* consequences. Condoms were important for sexual safety but they also weren't infallible. Sometimes they broke—and so did hearts. If Samantha had questions about sex, he'd like to think she'd bring them to him or, better yet, her mother. Instead, it seemed, she'd looked to a magazine for answers—the *wrong* answers.

And just what the hell was wrong with fairy tales anyway? He'd believed in a few of his own…once upon a time.

He tossed the magazine back into the drawer and closed it with a slam. If that was the kind of bullshit Samantha was reading, no wonder she seemed so pessimistic and depressed. The housekeeper ad he'd just rerun had better come through and fast. If not, he'd have to break down and go through a regular employment agency, though he didn't hold out much hope of finding *her* there, at least not in Washington, DC, because he wasn't just looking for a child care provider or a housekeeper or a cook, but some magical meshing of all three and more. What—no, make that *who*—he needed was a modern day fairy godmother, a woman not only young enough but also cool enough to connect with a jaded fifteen-year-old who'd spent most of her formative years in Manhattan. If she came with a magic wand, so much the better.

An automated ding drew his attention back to the laptop, where a new e-mail had just landed. Wanting to be done with work for the night, he clicked on the mailbox icon. The subject line, "Sweet and Old-fashioned," snagged his eye and piqued his curiosity. Another spam message advertising mail-order brides? It was most likely listener e-mail, although most people weren't that creative with their headers. Still, with time on his hands, he might as well open it.

DEAR DR. MANNON:

FOR THE PAST SEVERAL YEARS I'VE BEEN EMPLOYED AS AN AU PAIR IN MANHATTAN TO A FAMILY WITH TWO TEENAGE CHILDREN. MY EMPLOYERS ARE MOVING OVERSEAS TO UNDERTAKE MISSION WORK FOR THEIR CHURCH, AND HAVING JUST LEARNED THROUGH YOUR RADIO PROGRAM THAT YOU ARE SEEKING A HOUSEKEEPER/CHILDCARE PROVIDER, I'M INTERESTED IN DISCUSSING A POSSIBLE PLACEMENT IN YOUR HOME. I HOLD A BACHELOR'S DEGREE IN EDUCATION FROM THE CATHOLIC UNIVERSITY OF AMERICA AND WILL BE HAPPY TO PROVIDE ADDITIONAL REFERENCES UPON REQUEST.

P.S. I ABSOLUTELY *LOVE* YOUR PROGRAM!

The message was signed *Martha Jane Gray* and included a cell phone number with a Manhattan 212 area code.

Ross dragged a hand through his hair and tried not to get his hopes up, though the woman sounded promising. Hell, she sounded downright perfect. He read the e-mail again just in case he might have taken wishful thinking to the point of dreaming her up. Her bachelor's degree was in Education. She had experience dealing with teenagers. She lived in New York! The Manhattan address was sure to be a selling point with Sam, who had the attitude that anyone who lived farther out than Jersey City must be some kind of hay-chewing hick.

And to top it off, apparently her current employers were missionaries. That was just the kind of wholesome, positive influence he was looking to bring into his daughter's life.

Martha Jane Gray. Even her name seemed to carry him back to a kinder, gentler time. Already he was seeing her as some kind of cross between Julie Andrews from *Mary Poppins* and Juliet Mills from *Nanny and the Professor*—solid, serene...*magical.*

And yet in a world chock full of nuts, you couldn't be too careful, especially when bringing somebody into your home. First thing tomorrow he'd check her references, starting with a call to her current employers, the Swansons. One more phone call to her alma mater, Catholic University, and then assuming she came up clean, he'd arrange to bring her down to DC for a face-to-face interview. He'd be sure to have Sam come along as well. No matter how good Miss Gray might look "on paper," the tipping point would be how she handled herself with Samantha.

Ross reached for the computer's mouse. *Well, Miss Martha Jane, let's see what else you have to say for yourself.* Smiling for the first time that day, he clicked on the Reply icon and started typing.

Maybe it wasn't time to forget the fairy tale, or give up on the dream, just yet.

Chapter Two

Mannon's e-mail reply landed in Macie's inbox as she was rushing to her meeting with Starr. Skimming it from her phone, she held back a whoop. *Slam-dunk!* Her frog hadn't just taken the bait, he'd gobbled it hook and all, asking her to e-mail her resume and references as soon as possible. He'd signed off as *Ross Mannon*, no *Dr.* or *PhD* in the signature line, not that Macie was buying his just-folks humility act for a minute.

Now she had to sell the story to Starr. Walking the hallway to her boss's office felt a lot like walking the plank of a pirate ship. Other than her assistant editor, Terri, who managed a wobbly smile and a thumbs-up, none of her coworkers looked her in the eye as she passed. By the time she raised her fist to knock on Starr's closed door, she was primed to gnaw off all ten faux fingernails.

The brushed chrome handle slipped in her slick palm, but she managed to get the door open. Poking her head inside, she said, "You...er, wanted to see me?"

Cynthia Starling, known as Starr, looked up from the pile of layouts spread across her glass-topped desk, a scowl darkening her delicate porcelain features.

"That pulled ad hurt us in a major way. Beauté is one of our biggest accounts, not to mention our oldest. They've been with us since day one. Cultivating a new relationship to replace that lost revenue isn't going to happen overnight. Under the circumstances, it may not happen at all." She beckoned Macie inside with a toss of her shoulder-length, copper-colored curls.

Heart drumming, Macie pulled the door closed and crossed to the desk on Jell-O legs. She and Starr were friends outside of work but only to a point. Inside the office, her *friend* was all boss—and all business. "I know and I—"

"Sit down and listen up. I've spent most of my day upstairs getting my ass chewed out for giving you the go-ahead on that teen birth-control story."

Macie braced herself. *Here it comes, five years on staff flushed down the friggin' toilet.*

As if reading her thoughts, or maybe just her face, Starr said, "Relax, you still have a job. But any more sponsor calls like that and you'll be collecting unemployment, and I'll be right there with you."

So she was safe—for now. Weak with relief, Macie sank into one of a pair of vintage modern chairs positioned in front of the desk.

Perched on the edge of the cold chrome seat, she moistened her dry lips and prepared to make her pitch. "What would you say if I told you I thought I could pull off a story so high-profile, so hot, that Beauté will be calling us back, begging for space?"

Behind the round wire frames of her John Lennon glasses, Starr's eyes lit. "Go on."

Macie pulled her shoulders back from the tall girl slump she still sometimes fell into. "I'm thinking a celebrity profile, only with real teeth to it, an exposé, with a series of shorter outtake pieces to run as blog posts afterward to keep the momentum going. Something like, 'Ten Reasons Why This Guy Sucks' with every day's post building toward the big reveal. We could add a poll, too, really amp up reader engagement."

Starr cocked a ginger-colored eyebrow. "We're talking a big name?"

Macie drew a deep breath, readying herself to make her own big reveal. "Ross Mannon."

Starr's eyes widened, the black pupils nearly obliterating the aquamarine. "The conservative talking head who's made this an Extra Strength Tylenol day for me?"

"One and the same."

Starr eased back into her chair. "What makes you think he'll talk to you?"

Macie hesitated, then admitted, "Because he...uh...just e-mailed me back." She quickly rolled out the basics of what she was coming to think of as Operation Cinderella.

Starr took off her glasses and kneaded the bridge of her nose. "And you think that, after turning down a half dozen *Washington Times* reading women, he's going to open his door to you? I've seen your apartment, remember? You're no Martha Stewart."

Holding onto her game face, Macie shrugged. "He needs someone to drop off his dry cleaning and chauffeur his kid. How hard can that be? As for the cooking and cleaning, let's just say I have connections."

"Connections" came in the form of her college roommate, Stefanie, who lived in DC and owned a successful personal chef business. Good Enuf to Eat catered to dual career couples, delivering high-quality home-cooked meals hot to their doors.

Starr stabbed her expensive fountain pen behind one ear.

"How long are we talking?"

Always ask for more than you can hope to get. Macie swallowed against the dryness in her throat. "Two months ought to do it."

Starr snorted. "If 'it' involves driving *On Top* into the ground and me prematurely gray, then yeah, no problem." She drummed her fingers on the desktop. "Two weeks. It's the best I can do."

"Two weeks is barely enough time to unpack." Macie studied her own splayed fingers. Assuming Starr gave her the green light, the nail tips and multiple rings would have to go, as would her long hair, naval ring, and all-black wardrobe. "Six weeks including the two weeks of paid vacation I have coming to me. But if you end up running the story, and you will, I'll expect salary plus expenses."

Starr didn't rush to answer, a sign that her will was weakening. "Cocky little shit, aren't you?" she said after a moment, and Macie knew that those twitching lips meant she was struggling against smiling. "Okay, you get the six weeks, but you make sure to check in every frigging day by e-mail. Terri is a good assistant editor, but she's not ready to fly solo."

Adrenaline pumping, Macie shot up from her seat. "I'll get with Terri ASAP and make sure she has what she needs from me."

"Unless you're planning on knocking over an armored truck, see you keep your expenses within reason," Starr warned.

Turning to go, Macie grinned. "Hey, have you ever known me to be anything but reasonable?" It was a loaded question, and they both knew it.

She had one foot in the hallway when Starr called her back. Wondering if she might be reconsidering, Macie slowly turned around. "Yeah, boss lady?"

"Are you sure you know what you're doing?"

Macie hesitated. She was signing up to go undercover, not unlike feminist Gloria Steinem had done in the sixties, donning bunny ears and tail to infiltrate Hugh Heffner's Playboy Club. Only instead of a good girl playing at being bad, Macie would be a bad girl playing at being good. Could she really pull it off?

Mindful that she had not one but *two* people to convince, Macie concentrated on appearing confident and calm. "If everything goes according to plan, which it will, I'll have the research wrapped up and the finished story on your desk in four weeks, not six, which leaves Yours Truly with two solid weeks—with pay, thank you very much—to plant my winter-white ass on a patch of beachfront paradise." Backing out into the hall, she shot Starr a wink.

Screw a fairy godmother and pumpkin-pulling mice. The wheels of Operation Cinderella were already in motion and this coach was set to soar.

•

Going undercover as Mannon's personal Cinderella would call for an Oscar-worthy acting performance. To prepare for her starring role, Macie needed a major makeover. Fortunately, she was friends with Franc Whiting, an A-list Manhattan stylist. Frankly Franc had opened that summer in TriBeCa, and already getting an appointment with the owner involved a backlog of several months. Her panicked call to Franc's cell phone—"I need a fairy godfather *fast*"—scored her an after-hours appointment and the promise of a bottle of top-shelf pinot noir.

Hours later, she sat inside the renovated former warehouse facing a gilt-framed salon mirror, her hair hidden beneath the wrap of a fluffy pewter-colored towel. Grayish blue eyes stared back at her, heavily lined with charcoal-colored eye pencil, smudged to give her a smoky, slightly netherworldly look. A little pink around the whites—okay, borderline bloodshot—a sign her partying lifestyle was beginning to show. Naked lips, full thanks to Mother Nature and not collagen, and a dusting of pale powder completed the look she'd spent the past six months perfecting. Now, of course, it would all have to go.

Franc leaned in, his sculpted face joining hers in the mirror. "Courage, love. You're going to look amazing."

Macie wasn't sure why, but she always found his faux British accent incredibly soothing. "You always say that." Nervous, she fingered the edge of the towel.

The year before, she'd been a spiral-permed redhead with a penchant for eighties retro trash chic. Her current transformation, changing her hair from black to blond, was a grueling process involving stripping the black, bleaching to cover any residual brassiness, and then coloring the hair a wheat blond—the closest match to her natural shade, as far as she remembered. Between applications, she filled Franc in on Operation Cinderella. In a single breath, he'd declared her lunatic, outrageous, and, of course, brilliant.

"Voilà!" He swept away the towel and pale hair slid free.

Macie sucked in her breath, feeling as if she was staring at a stranger. "Wow, that's quite a…change." Though blond was her natural color, she'd been dyeing her hair darker for so many years now that she'd as good as forgotten what she used to look like.

Franc sent her a self-assured smile. "What can I say? False modesty isn't modesty at all and a frickin' fairy godfather couldn't have pulled this off in two hours." Pulling a black comb and scissors from the container of Barbacide solution set atop the black marble-topped counter, he addressed her reflection. "Speaking of fairy tales, don't you think that bit about your past employers being Christian missionaries might have been...well, a tad over the top?"

"Actually, I think he ate it up." Leaning back in the black, vinyl-covered chair while Franc gently combed out the tangles, she decided she'd better tell him the rest *before* he started with the scissors. "By the way, you'll probably be hearing from him soon."

The comb snared on a strand. Franc snapped up his head. "Why would I?"

Macie bit her bottom lip, wishing her glass of wine were within easier reach. "He asked me to e-mail him my references, and I couldn't risk giving him some bogus address and then having him find out, so I, er...gave him your and Nathan's landline." She cast a look behind to the curtained office where Franc's accountant and life partner was busy going over the books.

His perfectly plucked brows shot upward. "Nathan and I are supposed to be the Christian missionary couple you've been working for?"

She slipped her hand from beneath the smock and patted his bicep. "Relax, Brother Franc, it's no big deal. Your first name's the same only spelled with a *K*. All you have to remember is that you have a wife, Nadine, and two teenage kids."

He struck a pose reminiscent of Nathan Lane in the film version of *The Bird Cage* and batted his eyes. "Really, Macie, we're not drag queens. Nathan's falsetto is slightly superior to mine but still not terribly convincing."

Macie chuckled. "If he insists on talking to the wife, stall. Tell him she's out at a church bake sale or praying or... something, and then give me a buzz. My assistant editor, Terri, was a theater major at NYU. She can help us out."

The comb-out complete, he started dividing her hair into sections. "And what about our fictional children? Do the little darlings have names?"

Macie hesitated. "Chloe and, um…Zachary."

"Zachary, hmm, interesting choice." Looking ahead into the mirror, she caught him rolling his eyes at the mention of her on-again-off-again boyfriend. For the past two months, they'd been in the "off" phase—barring a few late night booty calls that he'd put out and she'd…answered.

Busted, she sunk down into her seat. "If I get stuck, it'll be easy to remember." Bringing the subject back around, she added, "Anyway, the four of you are about to set off for a two-year mission to… How does Belize sound? I know how you hate the winter in New York."

Running a hand through his mousse-spiked hair, he nodded. "Thoughtful. And who are you, by the way, or are Nathan and I the only ones with aliases?"

She tried out the guileless gaze and Stepford wife smile the good women of her hometown wore on a regular basis. Batting her eyes and stretching her lips to the limit, she drawled, "Why, I'm Martha Jane Gray, pleased to make your acquaintance."

Their eyes met in the mirror. "You sound terrifyingly authentic."

She hesitated, and then admitted, "I ought to. I grew up in a tiny town in Indiana called Heavenly."

"Sounds quite…bucolic."

She smothered a snort. Heavenly was an egregious misnomer. The town was home to a paper mill and was about as butt ugly as small town America got.

"It's prime Bible Belt territory. My folks were—are—thumpers from the old school. Living under their roof by their rules was the closest thing to doing time in a dungeon."

He paused in securing the last of the hair sections with a metal clip. "However did you escape?"

She rolled her shoulders, which suddenly felt as stiff as her neck. "I finally convinced them to give up on me."

He pulled the clip from a long swathe of hair and slid the comb through, stopping just below chin level. "Here?"

She swallowed hard, held her breath, and nodded. The scissors made their definitive cut, sealing the deal and sending a lock of wet hair sliding down the front of her smock like a tear.

He worked for several minutes in silent concentration. Macie tried to relax as a year's worth of hair growth fell to the tiled floor. Snipping away, Franc finally said, "I gather your parents don't approve of your lifestyle?"

She blew out a breath, amazed that after all this time it still hurt so much. "They don't approve of me period. New York City is just one big Sodom and Gomorrah as far as they're concerned, not that they'd ever venture out of the Heartland to come and see for themselves."

"That's too bad." He switched on the blow dryer, and she felt the bristles of the big rounded brush moving soothingly against her scalp.

Trying to relax, she closed her eyes while he rolled and unrolled chunks of her shorn hair to achieve maximum volume. Adieu to the days of letting her long locks dry naturally! The shorter, stylized cut would involve more upkeep, another sacrifice in the "line of duty."

Turning off the dryer, he said, "Snap to, Cinderella, and consider the magic wand waved."

She opened her eyes and looked into the mirror. "Oh, Jesus!" Even with her makeup unchanged, the woman who stared back didn't remotely resemble the one who'd first sat down mere hours earlier.

He set aside the styling tools. "I believe the appropriate exclamation in this case is bibbity boppity boo."

Biting her bottom lip, she reached up and touched her hair, which fell just below chin-level, a face-framing glossy cap. "I look like Martha Stewart."

Franc's flawless features relaxed into a grin. "I've always rather fancied the old girl. And you do have a certain country club vibe going on. With the right clothes and makeup, you can pull it off, love. You always do."

She gave her new 'do a test head shake. The precision-cut blond hair fell flawlessly back into place the moment the movement stopped. "It's a great cut, no doubt about that." She ran a hand through her hair and let it slide through her fingers. Despite all the chemicals, it felt remarkably silky, a testimony to the high-end products Franc used. "As long as a certain person approves, that's all that matters."

Franc held a hand over his heart. "Please, *please* tell me you're not speaking of Zachary."

She shook her head, noticing how the blond strands caught the light. "I meant Mannon, actually, but since you keep bringing him up, Zach does have his good points, you know."

Making a face, Franc reached for the open bottle of pinot set on the counter of the adjacent salon station and refilled their glasses. "And those would be fabulous abs and okay, a really tight butt, not that I was checking him out—I wasn't. I don't do grunge. But honestly, love, I wish you'd stop settling."

Accepting the glass, Macie snorted. "And hold out for Prince Charming?"

During her five years on the Manhattan singles' scene, Macie had become convinced that romance was the opiate of single women everywhere. Mr. Right simply didn't exist outside of fairy-tale fantasies. Anyone deluded enough to be waiting on Prince Charming had better get herself a vibrator and put herself on a Disney channel diet.

"You mock," Franc said, "but great guys are out there, I know they are. Take me for example — looks, personality, *and* brains, and did I mention I was spiritual?" He did a half turn, arms outstretched, wine slopping over the rim of his glass. Sucking the spillage from his knuckles, he met her gaze with his own suddenly serious brown eyes. "The complete package, Mace. That's what you deserve and nothing less."

She swung her head from side-to-side, getting used to the freedom of shorter hair. "I'm afraid there just aren't all that many straight guys out there who are complete packages." With the mainstay of her makeover behind her, she lifted her wineglass and took a sip.

He paused. "What about Ross Mannon? Does checking out his...*package* come as part of the assignment?"

Macie nearly squirted wine from her nose. Coughing, she said, "Are you kidding me? I may be dedicated — okay, borderline nuts — when it comes to my job, but even I'm not so out there that I'd prostitute myself to get a story."

Swirling the wine in his glass, he studied her. "That's some comfort, I suppose. Even though you must be borderline *something* to saddle yourself with a name like Martha... What was the other half?"

"It's Martha *Jane*, and I'll have you know it's my legal name." Seeing his jaw drop, she added, "If you don't believe me, I have the driver's license to prove it. I took Macie Graham as a pen name once I moved here, then I decided if I liked it so much why not use it all the time?"

If she'd stuck with Martha Jane Gray, she'd still be writing fluff pieces instead of covering the meatier, grittier assignments that had made her want to be a journalist in the first place. The name change had been powerfully symbolic of the fresh start she was making. It had meant putting to rest the naïve, altogether too trusting small-town girl she'd once been—forever.

Or so she'd thought.

For the next six weeks she'd signed herself up to not only walk the walk, but talk the talk of the very creature she'd sworn to never ever be—a sickeningly sweet, simpering old-fashioned girl. As transformations went, it amounted to Cinderella in reverse. But glancing down to the pile of hair at her feet, she told herself that no sacrifice was too great. She wanted to knock Prince Ross off his high horse once and for all. She wanted it bad. Galvanized to get going, she started up from the salon seat.

Franc's voice stayed her. "Not so fast. Nathan and I have a prezzie for you." Over his shoulder, he called loudly, "Nathan, love, pull your nose out of the Excel spreadsheets and come here. It's time."

Before she could ask what he was up to, he reached down into his styling station and withdrew what looked to be a vintage wooden shoebox. Straightening, he turned around and held it out to her.

Taking it and setting it in her lap, Macie was dumbfounded—and deeply touched. Being on the receiving end of a gift was never something she expected—or knew quite how to take. "What's the occasion?"

Franc shrugged. "No occasion. You've been such a supporter of the Salon, with all the fab coverage in *On Top*, and such a great friend to Nathan and me that when we saw these and heard the legend, we knew they were meant for you."

Shuffling out from the stockroom in a cardigan and khaki pants, a pen pushed behind one ear and a camera in hand, Nathan called, "Wait for me." Coming to stand beside Franc, he raised the camera. "Okay, open it."

Macie lifted the hinged lid to the camera's pop. Unfurling the tissue paper, she carefully took out one shoe. "Oh…my… God!"

The vintage ruby velvet-covered high heel was in mint condition and dated from the late thirties or early forties, Macie surmised, based on the styling and exquisite detailing. Amber crystals beaded the strap and the vamp above the peep toe, flashing like flawless canary diamonds.

Smiling broadly, Franc nodded. "Vintage Saks and first worn by the famous film star Maddie Mulligan. She had them on the night she received the news that she was nominated for an Oscar. That same night she received a marriage proposal from international financier Carlos Banks, her fourth and final husband."

"It was a classic case of opposites attracting," Nathan added, casting a fond look at Franc. "The Hollywood gossips of the day all swore it wouldn't last longer than any of Maddie's previous liaisons—only they couldn't have been more wrong."

A freak for black-and-white films, Macie was familiar with the legend. Maddie Mulligan had grown up poor in Dublin and made it rich in Hollywood during the early 1930s. After more than a decade of serial monogamy and gin-soaked partying, the famous film actress had settled down to an unexpected Happily Ever After with Banks, to whom she'd remained married for the rest of her life. Both in press interviews and in her memoir, she'd sworn her staid businessman husband was her one true love—and that the shoes had been her lucky charm.

"I snapped them up at a silent auction this summer," Franc said.

"At a charity event I had to drag him to," Nathan put in.

Franc declined to deny it. "We've been waiting for the right moment to give them to you. Given this is bon voyage for you and the launch for Operation Cinderella, what better time?"

Nathan's brow furrowed. "Bon voyage? Operation Cinderella? What have I missed?"

Franc tapped the shorter man's shoulder. "Macie's going to DC for a month or so. I'll fill you in later...*Nadine.*" Swinging back to Macie, he asked, "You like?"

"Like? I love! They're exquisite! I don't know what to say."

"Try them on," Nathan urged.

Willing her size seven-and-a-half feet to shrink to a seven, she kicked off her sling-back and slid her right foot into the red velvet. She'd expected some pinching, but the little slipper fit as if fashioned for her.

Dividing her gaze between her two friends and fairy godfathers, she wasn't sure what to say. "Thank you! I can't wait to wear them once I'm back in town."

Washington might be the nation's capital, but it was also a fashion wasteland. Besides, posing as Mannon's housekeeper and nanny likely wouldn't involve many opportunities for socializing, certainly not in formalwear.

Franc shook his head. "Take them with you and wear them even if it's just for yourself, as a reminder that you're still...well, *you*, a princess beneath the soot and cinders. Or in this case the Talbots and Burberry. Who knows, maybe some of Maddie's mojo will rub off."

Moved, Macie swallowed hard. "Okay. Thanks, guys, I will."

She'd given up on fairy-tale love pretty much by the time she'd boxed up her Barbie dolls. As for the legend, it was just that: a story, make-believe. Still, Franc had a point. Once she was in the throes of Operation Cinderella, it would be nice to have something of New York and her friends with her, something to remind her of who she was. A great pair of shoes was a great pair of shoes even if they didn't make it to any actual balls.

Chapter Three

"Hey, Mom, it's me." Cocking his head to the cell phone, Ross used his free hand to rinse his coffee mug at the kitchen sink.

"It's good to hear your voice, son," his mother said, as though it had been months since they'd spoken instead of last week. "How are you and Samantha getting along out there in Washington, DC?"

The way she said "Washington, DC" made the District sound like a foreign country. Then again, to his family back in Paris, Texas, it kind of was.

Ross hesitated. His folks knew Sam had come to live with him for a while, but that was all. He'd remained deliberately vague on the circumstances of her arrival, even though he suspected his mother wasn't fooled. "We're doing…well. I think I may have found a live-in housekeeper," he added, shifting the conversation to safer ground.

"That's wonderful. What's she like?"

"She's…" Opening the dishwasher, he set the used cup on the upper rack. "I haven't actually met her yet," he admitted. "I set up a lunch interview with her today. She's been living in New York, but she's from a small town in Indiana. She came east to study Education at Catholic University. So far we've only spoken on the phone."

He'd called Miss Gray at home three nights ago. What had started as a screening had carried into a conversation lasting almost an hour. A TV on in the background had prompted him to ask what movies she liked. As it turned out, they were both crazy about classic films. *North by Northwest* was one of her favorites, too. She considered Cary Grant the George Clooney of his day and Eva Marie Saint was "simply stunning." Colorizing original black-and-white films to make them more modern was "almost immoral." Ross had agreed wholeheartedly.

Before he'd known it, he was no longer leading an interview. He was engaging in a genuine conversation—and enjoying the hell out of himself. Sure, she'd been nervous at first, but the longer they'd talked the more she'd seemed to relax, revealing glimpses of warmth and intelligence and even humor.

His mother's voice drew him back to the moment. "You can tell a lot about a person's character over the phone. Not everything, but a lot. It's not always what they say but what they don't say that's the most telling," she added pointedly.

Closing the dishwasher door with his hip, Ross swallowed hard. Among the things he wasn't saying was that Sam was seeing a psychologist. Her regular weekly session was scheduled for that morning.

Sam chose that moment to stomp into the kitchen, a half-finished glass of orange juice in hand. Wearing a too-tight tank top and torn-at-the-knees low-rise jeans, she looked like she belonged on the back of a Hell's Angels hog, not in the exclusive private school where he'd enrolled her.

Memo to me: next time pick a school that requires students to wear uniforms.

She pushed past him to the sink and sloshed the leftover juice down the drain as though it cost pennies and not hard-earned dollars. Catching his eye, she said, "Chill, Daddy, I'll be ready to get my head shrunk in a few."

Ross covered a hand over the cell, hopefully in time to keep his mother from overhearing.

"Is that my darlin' grandbaby?" his mom asked, well knowing it was.

Shit. "Yes, ma'am, it is." Ross shot Sam a warning look and added, "Unfortunately, she can't talk right now. She has to go change…*immediately*." With his free hand he waved Sam out of the kitchen. "Listen, Mom, I…we've gotta run. I'll call you later, promise."

"All right, but you never did tell me her name."

"Her…?" Distracted by Sam, Ross took a moment before answering. "Oh, right, sorry. Martha Jane Gray."

"Martha Jane," his mother repeated, as if testing it out. "You don't hear old-fashioned names like that much anymore. I like the sound of it. I like the sound of her. I have a real good feeling about this young lady."

For the first time that morning, Ross felt himself smile. "Me, too, Mom."

• • •

The Northeast DC restaurant the Dubliner was on North Capitol Street, a few blocks from Union Station. The landmark Irish pub was operating at a low roar when Macie stepped inside, the wood-paneled bar looking very much as it had when she'd come with her college friends to hang out over pitchers of Guinness and bottles of Harp. A quick look around confirmed the lunchtime crowd consisted of the usual suspects, politicians and government workers from nearby

Capitol Hill, the men dressed in the DC "uniform" of dark suits or navy blazers and khakis, the women in neutral-colored suits or tailored separates. Similarly dressed in a tailored silk blouse and knee-length knit skirt, Macie walked up to the harried-looking young woman standing behind the hostess stand.

"Hi, I'm with the Mannon reservation."

The girl blew a russet-colored curl out of her eyes and glanced up from the messy stack of menus she'd been straightening. "Your party's already seated. I'll take you to the table in a sec, okay?"

A deep and now familiar baritone answered for her. "That's all right, Maag, I can take her."

Heart doing double time, Macie turned slowly around. Her gaze collided with a pair of impossibly blue eyes, and for a powerful few seconds, her tumbling heart seemed to spiral, then slip. "Dr. Mannon?" she said, finally finding her tongue.

"Ross." His deep voice, reminiscent of boots crunching on gravel, sounded slightly different in person than it had on the phone the other night; the telltale Texas intonation lengthening his vowels in a softer, less formal, sexier way. "You must be Miss Gray?"

Macie nodded, feeling her knees turn to wax—melting wax. "Y-yes, I'm she...I mean me." *Jesus, get a grip.*

After their phone conversation earlier in the week, she'd known she needed to put up a double-walled guard. The guy had been charming—but then she'd prepared herself for that. He was, after all, a media personality. That he was also majorly into classic movies had taken her by complete surprise. *North by Northwest* was his favorite film, too! Really, seriously! There'd been times during their almost hour-long talk when she'd found herself forgetting she was supposed to be acting out a role and had just been...herself.

That he was also "prettier" than his publicity picture was so not fair. Wearing a tweed blazer, comfortably worn jeans, and slightly scuffed Western boots, he might have walked out of the pages of an American Eagle Outfitters catalog.

She opened her mouth to invite him to call her Macie when she remembered where she was and, more importantly, who she was supposed to be. "Martha Jane." She hesitated, smiled, and stuck out her suddenly shaky hand.

"Pleased to meet you, ma'am." Holding her gaze, he slid his big hand around hers in a firm but not crushing grip.

Ma'am. Now there was a word she hadn't heard in a while, certainly not since the move to Manhattan. She glanced down at their joined hands, hers eclipsed by his broad palm and tapered fingers, and felt a spark somewhere between static electricity and lightning rush from her fingertips to her elbow.

Shivering, she pulled away and reached up to tuck a strand of hair behind her ear. "I hope I haven't kept you waiting?"

He shook his head. "Sam and I just got here a couple of minutes ago."

"Sam?"

"My daughter, Samantha."

"Oh, yes of course." Talk about blowing it off the bat.

"I had to take her out of school for a…doctor's appointment. Trip down go okay?" he asked, deftly turning the conversation back to her. Maybe her reporter's instincts were on hyperdrive, but he suddenly seemed on edge.

"It did, thanks. I love riding the train. It gives me a chance to read."

She started to bring up his book, but a tall teenage girl interrupted, sidling to Mannon's side. "Are we going to order or what? I'm starving." Hands stuffed into the pockets of her black Ducoti leather biker jacket, Samantha Mannon turned stony eyes on Macie.

Though they'd just met, Macie sensed the shift in Mannon. He turned toward the girl but not before Macie caught him wince. "Mind your manners, Sam. We have a guest." Expression shuttering, he looked back to Macie. "Miss Gray, this is my daughter, Samantha."

Macie held out her hand. "It's nice to meet you, Samantha."

"Sam," the kid corrected. Lip curled, she stared down at Macie's hand as though wondering when she'd last washed it.

Dropping her arm, Macie admitted the daughter wasn't at all what she'd expected. With her razor-cut medium brown hair, piercings, and torn-at-the knees jeans, Samantha Mannon looked more like a biker babe than the daughter of one of the country's leading conservative pundits.

Expression pained, Mannon gestured to a corner booth in the adjoining dining room. "We're just over there." He stepped aside, his hand brushing the small of Macie's back. The subtle guiding gesture sent her senses seesawing.

This is going to be a long six weeks, she thought, doing her best to fight the telltale tingling.

Praying she wouldn't tangle her feet or trip over a bump in the floor, she wove her way between tables and slipped into the high-backed booth. Samantha, not Mannon, took the seat directly across from her.

The girl's black-lined eyes, sharp as drill bits, bore into hers. "In case you haven't figured it out yet, Dad comes here every Friday for lunch, twelve o' clock sharp. You can set your clock by him…except for today. You made us late."

"Samantha!" Expression exasperated, Mannon took the seat beside his daughter.

Deciding she'd better start playing the part of the competent childcare worker sooner rather than later, Macie stepped in. "Actually, Samantha has a point. My train was running late. Where's Mussolini when you need him?" The Italian dictator's one positive was that he'd managed to keep the country's trains running on time—a first. Second to English, history had been Macie's favorite high school subject—before she'd stopped studying or caring about much of anything beyond getting by.

The kid's clueless look confirmed she'd never heard of Mussolini, but Mannon obviously had. He threw back his head and laughed, freeing them all from the tension of the moment and freeing something inside Macie, too. Startled by the sudden sense of well-being washing over her, she skimmed her gaze across his face, taking in the high brow and sculpted cheekbones, the creases at the corners of his eyes and mouth, and the hint of blond stubble on his jaw. That he wasn't totally clean-shaven as he'd been on the webcast was another surprise—and totally hot.

He glanced at Samantha, who was making a show of studying her menu. "Sam could use some help with World History—not her strongest subject, as you may have guessed." He followed the admission with a small, slightly crooked smile that had Macie's heart skipping beats. *Get a grip, Graham!*

"History sucks," Samantha announced, giving the menu an angry flip.

Opening her own menu, Macie hid a smile of her own. *Do your worst, kid. You might know the rules, but I wrote the book.*

A hassled-looking waitress materialized with a tray of ice waters. "Hi, my name is Michelle." She set the glasses down and looked to Macie. "May I start you off with a beverage?"

"An iced tea, please," Macie answered, hoping she didn't sound as sad about that as she felt. Back in New York, the only iced tea she drank was Long Island.

Mannon nodded. "I'll have the same, thanks."

The picture of seriousness, Samantha looked up and said, "I'll have a rum and Coke."

Mannon sighed. "Very funny, Samantha," he said and then to the waitress, "She'll have a regular Coke."

"A Diet Coke," Samantha corrected. Spotting her father's frown, she grudgingly added, "Please."

"I can take your order when I bring the drinks or, if you're ready now…"

Having spent the better part of her first year in New York supporting herself as a server, Macie recognized the broad hint. "I'm ready if you all are."

The menu featured hearty pub fare with several distinctive Irish dishes. Although she'd never been less hungry in her life, she settled on the Dubliner chicken salad, if only because managing a messy sandwich while fielding interview questions seemed too hard. Samantha ordered the house salad and fries, and Mannon the corned beef and cabbage along with a potato skin starter for them to share.

The waitress tucked the empty tray under her arm and darted away to another table. Macie looked across to Mannon and braced herself for the inevitable grilling to begin.

She didn't have long to wait. "I'm curious, Miss Gray, how'd you end up in New York from Indiana?"

So much for chummy chatting about black-and-white movies. Fortunately, once again, all she needed to do was stick to the truth. "Actually it was from Indiana to Washington, DC, for school, then from there to New York."

Mannon nodded. "Right, you majored in Education. How'd you come to pick that field, if you don't mind my asking?"

She hadn't picked it. Her college major had been foisted on her like everything else back then. The only way her parents would agree to foot the part of the tuition bill her partial scholarship hadn't covered was if she majored in nursing, library science, or education—the sole fields they considered suitable for a young woman now that Home Economics was no longer offered. She'd elected to study Education as the lesser of evils and then signed up for a second major in English, telling her parents it was the subject she wanted to teach; only staying confined inside a classroom was nowhere in her plans.

Ever since she could remember she'd wanted to be a journalist in the grand muckraking tradition of Upton Sinclair and Woodward and Bernstein, firing off scathing exposes calculated to make the big industry environmental polluters and corporate special interests quiver in their high-end boots. In the meantime, commercial magazine work paid the bills and racked up the bylines.

She took a drink of water. God but her throat was dry. "My mother taught kindergarten before she married Dad, so I suppose working with kids is sort of in my blood."

He rested his folded hands atop the table, and Macie felt her gaze drawn downward. Golden hairs dusted the broad backs, and the interlocked fingers exuded harnessed strength—power. Scarring thickened the flesh over the knuckles. Mannon had once worked with his hands doing hard labor: yet another surprise.

"Your practicum was in Early Childhood Education and yet in your e-mail you said the family you just got through working for has teenagers."

She snapped up her gaze. "Yes, that's right, although Chloe was in middle school when I started." Chloe was the name she'd picked for her future daughter back when she'd still believed in real-life Happily Ever Afters. "I've found that teens are the age group I enjoy working with the most."

He regarded her beneath a slightly raised brow. "Why is

that?"

Damn, why couldn't she have kept K.I.S.S. sacred? Stalling, she sipped more water. "Well, I suppose because it's… it's such a confusing time for kids and yet a magical one, too. Or at least it should be. Watching them transform into young adults and helping them make that transition successfully is something I find really challenging but really rewarding, too." She thought about tossing in a butterfly analogy but then reminded herself that when it came to lying, less really was more. "And I suppose I have a personal stake, too."

"How's that?" His voice hadn't raised so much as a decibel and yet she sensed the shift in him, the wariness.

She answered honestly. "My sister, Pam, is a sophomore in high school. If nothing else, I suppose that brings home to me just how hard it is to be a kid these days."

She hadn't seen Pam since her last disastrous trip home for the holidays nearly two years ago. The fireworks she and her folks had raised had made it feel more like the Fourth of July than Christmas. Her dad had accused her of ruining the holiday for everyone by leaving early, but cutting out before the situation got any worse had seemed like the best present she could give all of them, herself included.

The lump lodging at the back of her throat warned it was time to get a lot less real. "But look at me going on and on when you're the one who's literally written the book on the subject." She reached into her leather bag and pulled out the hardback she'd brought along.

Raising Sane Kids in an Insane World wasn't going to put Nora Roberts out of business, but the prose was livelier and better crafted than she'd expected. For an academic, Mannon wasn't a half bad writer, assuming he hadn't hired someone to ghost. Regardless, his thinking was all wrong.

"I finished it on the trip down. I was hoping you might

autograph it for me—if it's not too much trouble."

Silent until now, the kid rolled her eyes and hissed, "Suck up," beneath her breath.

Ignoring her, Macie slid the book across the table toward Mannon.

She'd expected him to preen but if anything he looked almost...embarrassed. "Sure, I'd be happy to."

He pulled an expensive looking fountain pen from his jacket pocket, along with an eyeglass case, and opened the book to the title page. When he slid on the wire frames, Macie found herself forgetting to breathe. She'd never before thought of glasses as sexy, but on Ross Mannon, they definitely were. The scratching of the pen across the page filled the silence, and Macie was grateful for the time to gather herself. She took another long drink of water, feeling as though she'd just logged in too many minutes in a sauna—dry-mouthed and lightheaded enough to make her glad she was sitting down. When she looked up, she caught the kid smirking. If a fifteen-year-old could see through her it was obvious she was blowing this interview big time.

"Here you go." He pocketed the pen and handed her the closed book.

"Thank you." She tucked the signed book back into her bag just as their waitress returned with their drinks and appetizer.

Samantha took one look at the plate of stuffed skins and shoved it away. "They have bacon on them. I hate bacon. Chopped up chunks of some poor innocent pig—gross!"

"Suit yourself." Mannon offered the plate to Macie. "Samantha sees herself as a vegetarian, except she eats raw fish. Go figure."

The girl glared at him. "I *am* a vegetarian and the sushi I eat is the veggie kind."

Why she felt the need to intervene Macie couldn't say, but staring back into Samantha's face, the angry eyes suspiciously bright, something touched her. The tough act was just that, an act, and having once been in a similar place, she couldn't stop wondering what exactly Samantha Mannon was working so hard to wall herself off from.

In a show of solidarity, she admitted, "I don't eat much pork myself, but look, it's just sprinkled on the top. You can pick it off. I'm going to." To demonstrate, she served herself a potato wedge and brushed off the crumbled bacon with the tines of her fork.

Samantha watched with narrowed eyes, and then with the suddenness of a rainbow appearing, she snapped upright. "That's a great idea." Beaming, she reached for the plate and served herself not one but two skins. Dodging her father's scowl, she ignored her cutlery and brushed off the bacon with her fingers. "Miss Gray, would you please pass me that ketchup over there?"

"Certainly." Macie handed her the bottle, wondering if the kid might be bipolar and her meds had just now kicked in.

Samantha twisted off the cap and upended the bottle over her plate. "Sure is slow." She slapped at the glass bottom.

Mannon reached for the condiment. "Here, honey, let me help you."

Holding the uncapped bottle at an angle, Samantha shook her head. "No thanks, Daddy, I've got it."

Macie looked up just as the ketchup missile struck, a sloppy wet scarlet slap on her left breast.

"I am *so* sorry, Miss Gray." Gaze glittering, Samantha plunged a napkin into her water glass and popped up from her seat toward Macie.

"Oh, no you don't…I mean, no thanks. I can take it from here." Macie snatched the dripping napkin out of the kid's hand.

"Samantha, sit down." Mannon's command, edged with real anger, had his daughter dropping back into the booth.

"Gosh, I hope that isn't real silk." The kid could barely stifle her smile.

The tailored blouse was not only 100 percent silk but also one of Macie's recent purchases from Ann Taylor—and not from the sale rack. Using what was left of the water in her glass to dampen a corner of her napkin, she caught the glob before it could drop into her lap and take out her skirt, too.

Blotting the stain and gritting her teeth, she forced herself to say, "Don't worry about it, Samantha. *Accidents* happen."

Accident, my ass. The little monster had meant to slime her, taking aim with the precision of a paintball enthusiast. Macie met Mannon's gaze. Beneath the obvious parental mortification laid a fleeting look of fear. *He knows she did it on purpose, too, and he's asking himself what that means.*

He shook his head, looking so stressed she almost felt sorry for him—almost. "I'm terribly sorry, Miss Gray. Send me the dry cleaning bill and I'll take care of it. Better yet, let me replace it."

"Thank you, but that won't be necessary."

Surveying the damage, she saw the water had rendered her plunging white silk push-up more or less transparent. Her shirt stuck to her skin, showing through to the lace edging of her bra and perhaps to her "true colors," too. The bra and panties were the only clothing articles on her body that still let her be herself. She'd thought expressing herself through sexy underwear would be safe. Not so much, it seemed.

"Look, Daddy, its soaked right through to her…uh…bra." Samantha's gaze shot from Macie's boobs back to her face. Flicking aside messy bangs, she added, "Don't you worry, Miss Gray, you tell us your size, and we'll pick you up a nice new one from the Victoria's Secret over there in Union Station, won't we, Daddy?"

"Samantha, settle down!" Mannon, his color high, grabbed for the girl's arm, pulling her back down into the booth when she would have risen.

Taking in the byplay, Macie decided Samantha Mannon was either the biggest brat on the planet or a poster child for Ritalin—only time would tell. Either way, having your kid mouth off in public before a total stranger would try the patience of any parent, but for a self-styled child-rearing expert like Ross Mannon it must be torture—or in this case, just desserts. So why couldn't she shake feeling sorry for him?

Macie was about to excuse herself to the ladies' room when the waitress showed up with their meals. She took one look at Macie's blouse and promised to bring back some club soda for the stain.

Macie looked down at her lunch of lettuce heaped with strips of hot fried chicken, olives, and hardboiled egg, and felt her stomach flip. The prospect of spending the next six weeks in the thick of the Mannon family's dysfunction suddenly seemed a lot more like enrolling in boot camp than taking on a journalistic assignment.

Mannon didn't look so hungry himself. "I'm going to get you that club soda." He whipped the napkin off his lap, tossed it on the seat, and slid out of the booth.

Across from her, Samantha attacked her fries with the gusto of a reality TV contestant who'd lived off worms for weeks. Left alone with her, Macie couldn't resist asking, "Aren't you forgetting the missing ingredient?" She tapped the ketchup bottle with her newly shortened, clear-polished nail.

The kid looked up, gaze glinting with what must be pure evil. "No thanks. I never touch the stuff."

•

"Sundaes for dessert, Miss Gray? Only, if Samantha asks for the bottle of chocolate syrup, I'd think twice," Mannon said with a chuckle, pushing his cleaned plate to the side.

Macie felt herself smiling back. Since returning with club soda and extra napkins, her prospective employer had managed to restore them to good spirits—everyone but Samantha.

"Duly warned," she answered, cutting the kid a look.

Sullen gaze on her picked-over plate, Samantha didn't join in, not that Macie expected otherwise. Clearly her plan to sabotage the interview had failed—so far. If anything, the ketchup incident had leveled the playing field. Macie felt sure Mannon would have questioned her more closely if it hadn't been for his daughter's bad behavior. Far from grilling her, he seemed to be pulling out all the stops on the charm while keeping his gaze trained on the terrain *above* her shoulders. Once or twice, though, she thought she'd caught that deep blue gaze dipping. That he might be checking her out, not as a housekeeper or nanny but as a woman, should have offended her. It should have…only it didn't. Then again, her whole purpose in coming here was to prove he wasn't the squeaky clean conservative he portrayed. If showing him her chest hastened that happening, then she'd gladly spring for Samantha Mannon's next piercing—and toss in a dragon tattoo.

After paying the bill, Mannon looked at her and said, "I'd like to swing by the apartment and give you a quick tour, if that's okay. That way you can check out the place for yourself and evaluate the perks."

"The perks?" she echoed, wondering what she'd missed.

He nodded. "My TV flat screen is a full sixty-five inches and my cable package is deluxe. It includes the classic film channel, I swear it," he added with a smile.

She might be dressed like an angel but thinking of Mannon in terms of "inches" and "packages" had her demon heart beating double time. And though warmed by his reference to their unexpectedly delightful phone chat about old movies — Zach had refused to watch anything older than the eighties — it was clear there was only one answer she could give.

"Sure, I'd like that. I turn into a pumpkin at five, though, when my train leaves." She'd bought her return ticket in advance and not only because it was cheaper. Since launching Operation Cinderella, like that fairy-tale princess, she always had an eye on the exit.

"Don't worry," he assured her, "I promise I'll have you back in plenty of time."

They left the restaurant and headed to Union Station, where Mannon's car was parked, Samantha straying ahead. Glad to be outside again, Macie savored the sunshine on her face. Unlike urban dense Manhattan, DC boasted ample open space as well as warm weather for much of the year.

She'd fallen in love with the capital city when she'd first arrived as a freshman. Had it really been eight years? Biking along the Potomac, picnicking beneath the cherry blossoms, seeing the restored *Lawrence of Arabia* at Cleveland Park's iconic Uptown Theater were fond if faraway memories.

The light changed to "No Walk," and they halted at the curb. Mannon asked, "You come back here much?"

She turned and looked up at him. Even tall and wearing heels, she was shorter than him by several inches. "This is the first time I've been back since graduation," she admitted. "I suppose I'm a little lost in nostalgia."

One corner of his mouth kicked up in a sexy half smile

and his deep blue gaze fixed on her face. "You strike me as kind of young for nostalgia."

She caught his amused expression and tried to feel pissed-off, but it was no use. He was too freakin' charming, too unflappably good-natured. "It depends on how you measure time, I guess."

His gaze lingered for a moment more, the unblinking brush of his blue eyes doing funny, fluttery things to her insides. "I reckon you have a point."

Reckon. Exactly when had she landed smack dab in the middle of a *Bonanza* re-run? But delivered in his slow, syrupy drawl, the quaint expression sounded not so much out-of-touch as sexy.

Very sexy.

Ahead, a scowling Samantha slouched at the fountain in front of the station, shifting from foot to foot in obvious impatience. A shadow crossed his face. "Sometimes I look at Sam, and I can't figure out where the years have gone. Other times, I feel the weight of every day like it's a year."

According to his website bio and Wikipedia entry, he was thirty-four, eight years older than she. Still, thirty-four was young. It seemed, though, that he must not feel it. "I know," she found herself admitting, and the weird thing was she actually *did* know. She might be newly twenty-six, but since turning sixteen and coping with all the crap that had gone down during that pivotal, disastrous year, she'd felt older than her age—a world-weary soul locked inside a young woman's body. Wearing edgy clothes and makeup was like putting a patina over the pain—it held in the hurt but also kept more from seeping in. Now and for the next six weeks, that buffer would be gone.

The walk sign flashed on, and they crossed. Samantha flew away from the flagpole and bolted over to her father.

"Daddy, there's a sale on at Express. I really need — "

"Absolutely nothing." She started to object, but he cut her off with a shake of his head. "Your room's packed so tight, stuff's spilling out into the hallway. You clean up that mess and then *maybe* we'll talk about shopping."

Samantha sputtered a "so not fair" and stalked off. Watching her head for the ramp leading to the parking deck, Mannon turned to Macie. This time his smile didn't come close to reaching his eyes. "Speaking of nostalgia, would you believe, Miss Gray, that my daughter was once the sweetest child on God's green earth?"

Macie resisted the urge to reach up and lay a comforting hand on that broad and obviously burdened shoulder. "Weren't we all, Dr. Mannon?"

•

They caught up with Samantha at Mannon's white Ford Explorer in an upper tier of the station's garage. Once they cleared the deck and turned onto Massachusetts Avenue, they made it to the Watergate in less than twenty minutes despite the heavy traffic. Macie had to admit she was impressed, as much by Mannon's choice of unpretentious vehicle as by his urban driving skills. So far nothing about him was as she'd expected. In light of her mission, that wasn't necessarily a good thing.

He swung into his reserved space in the condo's underground garage, got out to open Macie's passenger side door, and then led the way to the elevator for his eastside tower apartment.

"Home, sweet home," he said, opening the condo's door.

Macie stepped inside the cool, marbled foyer. "This is beautiful," she said, trying not to gawk. "And what a great location."

She glimpsed a dining room of gleaming, wide-planked wooden floors and high ceilings offset with crown molding. A sunken great room led off from the eating area. Carpeted in wall-to-wall plush beige, it was furnished with an overstuffed leather sectional sofa, matching chairs, and a glass-topped coffee table. True to Mannon's word, a huge wall-mounted flat screen TV dominated the living area. Drawn drapes revealed sliding glass doors and, beyond them, a bird's eye view of the Kennedy Center. Spewing conservative doctrine was some cash cow. The place must have cost a mint.

He tossed the car keys on the hallway table. "I'm still getting used to the feeling of being hemmed in."

Macie swallowed a snort. Hemmed in! Her six hundred square foot East Village studio walkup could fit comfortably inside his foyer. Rather than say so, she turned to study an abstract landscape, the oil-on-canvas covering most of the far wall. Other than a few framed photos set about, the main rooms were devoid of dust-collecting decorative items, which should make them easier to keep clean.

Mannon called out to Samantha, who'd drifted into the living room, the TV remote already in hand. "I need to talk to Miss Gray—in private."

Macie looked up and saw Samantha shrug. "Knock yourselves out." She dropped the remote and stomped toward a hallway. Seconds later a door slammed.

Mannon kneaded the bridge of his nose. His eyes, Macie observed, looked tired as well as a shade lighter than earlier. Once again she was hit by the powerful pull to somehow make things better for him. But making Ross Mannon feel better, no matter how personable and charming and, okay, *hot* he was in person, didn't come close to aligning with her Operation Cinderella mission.

He gestured her to the sofa. "Have a seat, Miss Gray. Can I get you something—coffee, tea, a Coke?"

A tequila shot, I'm thinking. The gravity of his tone stripped away her confidence and sent her stomach sinking. Had she overreacted to the ketchup incident or hadn't she reacted enough? Afterward, had she talked too much or too little? She looked into his eyes and the shadows she saw brought back a montage of her life's low points since high school, from when she'd repeatedly "failed to live up to her potential" to all the times since when she'd just plain failed.

Standing in the shadow of the oversized painting, she shook her head. "No thank you."

"Mind if I make some coffee for myself?"

Actually she did mind, she minded a lot. If he was going to give her the thumbs-down, she'd just as soon have it over with so she could get the hell out of there and back to Manhattan where she belonged. But the choice wasn't hers.

"Go ahead...please." Dropping her bag, she followed him out to the galley-style kitchen and took a seat on one of the high-backed breakfast bar stools.

He puttered about, opening and closing cabinet drawers, swearing beneath his breath when he couldn't find the coffee filters. Looking up from the silverware drawer he'd rifled through, he said, "You sure I can't get you something?"

Antsy with impatience, Macie shook her head. "Dr. Mannon, if you have something to say to me then please just come out and say it."

"You're right." He put down the coffee scoop and faced her. "Above all, I want to apologize for my daughter's behavior. There's no excuse for that kind of rudeness."

Unused to being on the receiving end of a man's apology, she wasn't sure how to react. "Sam is obviously going through a difficult time." Christ, that was just the kind of lame platitude she'd come to hate.

He let out a heavy breath. "I'm afraid there's more to it than that." He carried the coffee pot to the sink. Running the tap, he said, "I wouldn't want this to become common knowledge, but Sam's living with me because she ran away from her mother's in Manhattan."

The revelation tripped Macie's mind back to the times when *she'd* run away. Two months shy of seventeen, she'd gotten halfway to Chicago when the car ran out of gas and she'd had to stop and refill it using her dad's credit card. By then her parents had put a tracer on the card, which was how the police had caught up with her and hauled her back home. The next time, she'd made sure to take along what to a sixteen-year-old had seemed like plenty of cash. It wasn't. She hadn't made it to Chicago that time, either.

She found herself saying, "When a child runs away, there's almost always a reason." Who knew, Samantha's reason might well be the crux of her juicy tell-all for *On Top*.

He crossed back to the granite counter and poured water into the well of the Mr. Coffee. Measuring out the grounds, he said, "I agree. Unfortunately whenever I try to get her to tell me what went wrong, she freezes up and threatens to run away—textbook emotional blackmail, and, by the way, it's working." He punched the switch on the coffeemaker and turned to face her.

Stunned by the raw vulnerability she read on his face, she worked to keep her expression neutral and her sympathy in check. "At least she felt like she could come to you," she said, hoping to draw him out about his divorce. "She must trust you on some level."

He dragged a hand through his thick blond hair, and she found herself wondering if it felt as soft as it looked. "Up until a year ago we had a damn good—excuse me—good relationship. Now I just don't know. The school counselor back in New York seems stumped, too. She recommended Sam see a psychologist. That was the doctor's appointment we came from earlier." He punctuated the admission with a shake of his head. "At this point, I feel like Ozzy Osbourne's a better parent than I am. He may have beheaded bats and urinated on a monument honoring the Alamo's fallen, but he's also stayed married to his second wife for three decades and his kids and grandkids worship him. Maybe I should see if he'll sub for me while I go off and figure out this parenthood stuff."

She hadn't expected him to be so heart wrenchingly humble, so scathingly self-honest. Certainly she hadn't expected him to have an actual sense of humor! The words *complete package* came to mind but she shoved them aside. She couldn't afford to let herself like Ross Mannon. More than any other foreseeable flaw in her plan, liking this man would seriously mess with her mission—and her mind.

"Dr. Mannon, why are you telling me all this?"

He didn't hesitate. "Because I want to be upfront with you about what you're signing up for if you accept this position."

Heart drumming, she asked, "Are you saying the job is mine if I want it?"

His gaze, disarmingly earnest, met hers. "Yes, Miss Gray, that's exactly what I'm saying." One corner of his mouth lifted in the sexy half smile that in the course of the afternoon had come to feel so very familiar. "The question is what do *you* say?"

Her fluttery stomach stilled, her heart lifted. Ross Mannon was hiring her! Operation Cinderella was taking off! Whatever test he'd put her to, she'd apparently passed—with flying colors. With his gaze holding hers, she felt as if the magic wand was being waved, the coach rolling forward. Suddenly life was, if not exactly enchanted, good again for the first time in a very long while.

She smiled and stuck out her hand. "How soon can I start?"

Chapter Four

Macie had returned to New York that evening and gotten directly to work—packing. Once she had, all the moving parts of Operation Cinderella had fallen into place as if by magic. Her assistant editor, Terri, had just split with her roommate and was looking for a short-term place to stay. In exchange for watching her apartment, taking care of Stevie, and keeping her lone plant alive, Macie had handed over the keys rent-free. Even packing, which she'd dreaded, had proven a cinch. Except for her laptop, new clothes, and what she'd come to think of as her red Cinderella slippers, there wasn't much else she needed to bring.

Saying good-bye to friends was a lot harder. Franc and Nathan had treated her to dinner at her favorite Murray Hill Indian restaurant on her last night in town. She used her morning train as an excuse to make an early night of it, but the truth was she wanted to log in some quality snuggling time with Stevie, AKA Stevie Wonder, before leaving. Since she'd sprung him from the city shelter last year, they'd been pretty much inseparable. A scraggly adult street cat with one eye missing and the other badly infected, he'd been deemed "unadoptable" and slated for euthanasia. Fortunately, the euthanasia tech had called in sick the day Macie had walked by after work. She'd taken one look at Stevie, crawling to the front of his rusted metal cage to butt his little black-and-white head against her hand, and had fallen head-over-heels.

Too bad it wasn't that easy with men.

Sitting in a coach class Amtrak car bound back for DC, she acknowledged that D Day had arrived. There was nothing left to plan and a hell of a lot yet to do. Lost to her thoughts, the three-and-a-half-hour train trip slipped by.

This time Stefanie met her at the gate. Her dark hair gathered into a thick braid and a baggy sweater and jeans covering her curvy figure, Stef hadn't changed much since their college days. Obviously the same couldn't be said for Macie. Stef would have walked past if Macie hadn't reached out and tapped her on the shoulder.

Staring from behind tortoiseshell framed glasses, Stef said, "Mace? Is that you?"

"In the freakin' flesh." Macie let go of her suitcase handle and opened her arms.

They hugged, and suddenly it was as if they were back in college, roomies and best friends forever. Pulling back, Stef gave her a friendly once over. "You look great. The last time I saw you, your hair was…magenta, I think."

Macie grinned. Being a style chameleon was a point of pride. "What can I say? I like to keep my friends on their toes."

"Your e-mail said you're here for six weeks on some kind of undercover assignment. It must be pretty high end to require a personal chef."

Macie spotted a Starbucks. "How about I buy you a coffee and we can talk about the details?"

Stefanie smiled. Along with sweets, caffeine was her weakness. "Make it a tall mocha with whip and you've got yourself a deal."

A few minutes later, settled in at one of the café tables with her luggage crowded around them, Macie ran down the basics of Operation Cinderella.

Not surprisingly, Stef seemed more than a little shocked. "Okay, let me see if I get this straight. You're going to move into this guy's home by pretending to be his housekeeper and then snoop around until you dig up enough dirt to make it newsworthy?"

Macie nodded. "Basically, yes." Hearing it from her friend's lips, her mission didn't sound especially noble.

Stef licked a dab of whipped cream from the corner of her mouth before answering, "Look, Mace, you know I'm the last one to rain on your parade, but how do you plan to pull this off? The last time I visited you in New York, you had a six-pack of Diet Coke and a jar of mayonnaise in your fridge— and the mayo had expired."

"That's where you come in."

"So you need me to be your shadow chef," Stef said.

Macie nodded. "The building has a service elevator. We just need to smuggle you and the food up without being seen. Mannon e-mailed me a copy of his weekly schedule and from what I can tell he's a creature of habit. During the week, he's at work until six, and the kid is enrolled in prep school, plus she's signed up for a shitload of extracurricular activities that'll keep her out of the condo. We just need to work out a system where you drop off dinner by, say, four o'clock, and then I warm it up later."

Stef's eyes widened. "That's at least two hours between delivery and serving! It's really hard to keep meat from drying out, and sauces get lumpy once—"

"Hey, he's not expecting Emeril, just someone who can cook the basic dishes."

Stefanie sighed. "But food, even simple food, is so much more than sustenance. Eating is a sensual, social experience. A communion that engages the body and soul…"

Macie sipped her soy latte and let her friend rhapsodize. For Stefanie Stefanopoulos food wasn't just food. It was passion. Macie had listened to various versions of this lecture for the four college years she and Stef had roomed together. Ordinarily a rule-abiding good girl, Stefanie had smuggled a hot plate and microwave into their dorm room and had used the contraband equipment to create savory snacks from odds-and-ends pilfered from the dining hall or purchased from a nearby convenience store. Now equipped with a state-of-the-art commercial kitchen and the finest farm-to-table ingredients, Stef should have been living a gourmet fairy tale—except there was no prince to partake of her fabulous feasts, only her widowed father and his second family: a step-monster and her two surly gremlin girls, all perennially on various dreary diets.

"What about the weekends?" Stef asked.

Macie hesitated. "I'll have to figure that part out once I'm there, but I'm guessing he probably works a lot, maybe even goes into the office for a few hours. If he were home, he wouldn't need to hire someone to keep tabs on his kid, would he? And what kid on the planet doesn't like pizza? Oh, by the way, she's a vegetarian."

"Good to know." Stef eyed her. "Are you sure you know what you're doing?"

"No," Macie admitted, "but that never stopped me before. And this time I have a budget to back me up. I'll pay you double your regular fee."

"Thanks, but don't worry about it. I always end up making too much of everything anyway. Maybe your magazine could make a donation to the homeless shelter where I usually drop off the extra food?"

Macie beamed. She couldn't vouch for *On Top* but she would make the donation herself. "Consider it done!" Taking down a major conservative pig *and* feeding people. Operation Cinderella was turning into a mission of mercy all around.

"Before I forget…" Stef reached inside her pocket and pulled out a white business card bearing the logo of a dancing broom. "A friend of mine runs a housecleaning service. Her crew does an excellent job and her people are all super trustworthy. Tell her I referred you, and she'll give you a discount."

Macie took the card and dropped it inside her bag. "Thanks, Stef, you're the best. I only have one more question."

Stef grinned. "Let me guess. What's for dinner?"

·

Mannon had arranged for Macie to pick up a spare key at the front desk. She made a mental note to have copies made for Stef and the housekeeping service and then headed for the elevator. A uniformed doorman with a broad, pleasant face and white hair took charge of her luggage, steering her toward the resident lift. She tipped him a five, wondering if that was not enough, too much, or just about right. For a while now, she'd fantasized about what it would be like to live in a doorman building. Now that she was, for the next six weeks at least, she felt shy about it.

Mannon's handwritten note left out on the breakfast bar informed her that he'd be home at seven and that Sam was spending the night at a friend's house to give her the evening to settle in. *Considerate*, she thought, and then told herself not to get bogged down by the sentiment. In all likelihood he'd made his plans for his convenience, not hers.

She wandered about the condo, running her fingertips over counters and furnishings, imprinting the layout of hallways and rooms, the texture of fabrics and the placement of fixtures in her mind. The rooms were so spacious, the ceilings so high it was hard to believe she was in an apartment at all.

She opened a door and instantly knew she'd stumbled onto Samantha Mannon's room. It hadn't been on the other day's tour and now she saw why. Brimming with typical teenage clutter, it had all the usual adult crazy-makers—an unmade bed, piles of dirty clothes, and a damp bath towel scattered about. The mess didn't bother Macie, but she supposed she'd have to get on the kid's case if only for show.

She messaged Stef to let her know she could safely push the dinner delivery as late as six, and then went to her room, an airy, pleasant space she'd glimpsed on her previous visit. The queen-sized iron bed was covered with a simple white duvet, the hardwood floor with a floral print area rug. The white shabby chic dresser and matching night table were devoid of decorative items. Roman shades dressed the double window. The latter looked out onto an interior courtyard, not the city skyline, though of course she was only "the help." But as far as she was concerned the very best feature of her new accommodations was the en suite full bath. Being undercover was one thing, living with the subject of your investigation twenty-four-seven entirely another. Even Woodward and Bernstein had gotten to go home at night. The prospect of jostling for morning shower time with Samantha Mannon or her father, for that matter, had been worrisome, she admitted now. Bonus: she wouldn't have to bother running out for a nightlight. She could sleep with the bathroom light on, as she did in her apartment at home.

She hung her clothes in the walk-in closet, laid her folded

things in the white dresser, and stowed her shoes, including the boxed vintage red heels, on the closet floor. Lastly she set Stevie's framed holiday photo with "Santa Paws" on her night table. Tamping down a twinge of homesickness, she decided to relax with a shower.

Staring into the steamed bathroom mirror sometime later, a fluffy white bath towel wrapped about her freshly washed hair, she drew a deep breath. The worst was over. She was here. She'd made it. Now all she had to do was be a good undercover reporter, which in this case meant slipping into the skin of the sweet, old fashioned girl she was pretending to be and staying there for the next six or so weeks. For some, that might seem like a tall order.

For Macie, being someone else was what she did best.

• • •

Ross entered the apartment at a quarter to seven, thrumming with a vague yet persistent impatience. Even if he hadn't stopped to confirm the new arrival with his doorman, the amazing smells wafting from his kitchen announced that he and Sam were no longer living alone. Martha Jane Gray had arrived.

She met him in the living room, looking fresh and pretty in a cool cotton floral print he knew was called a sheath only because his ex was a fashion photographer and a committed clotheshorse.

"You're home early."

Her slightly husky tone had him thinking of sex, specifically the aftermath of sex, when bodies were sated and sheets damp and there wasn't much left to say because it had all been said already—with actions not words. Sex might not be a distant memory exactly, but it had been a while since he'd had a woman in his life. Seeing Miss Gray moving about his home turf as though she lived here, which as of now she did, had him thinking it might be time to get back in the game — with someone closer to his age whom he didn't employ.

Grateful she couldn't read minds, he set down his case. "The four o'clock staff meeting that always starts closer to five and never ends before seven was canceled." He dropped the button fronting his navy blazer, eager to be free of the thing. "How was your trip down?" He was genuinely interested, but also desperate to distract himself from how delectable she looked and smelled and, no doubt, tasted. *Bad Ross, really bad!*

"Good, thanks." She moved toward him, her chin-length hair a glossy blond frame for her face, which wore just the slightest trace of blush and pale pink lipstick. "Allow me," she said, slipping behind him.

Female hands, light and competent, settled briefly on his shoulders, helping him off with the coat, an old-fashioned civility that hardly anyone practiced anymore. Taken by surprise, Ross tried again not to think about how good she smelled — was that really just soap and shampoo? — or the magic her slender fingers might work on other, more sensitive spots.

She stepped back around to his front, the garment draped over her slender forearm. "Dinner will be ready in a bit. I hope you like pot roast."

Ross didn't like pot roast. He loved it. "I didn't expect you to cook on your first night," he said despite being pleased that she had. She dismissed the notion with a breezy wave of one slender, subtly manicured hand. "Cooking helps me settle in. I'll call you when it's ready if that's all right?"

Ross nodded. "Great, I'll be in my study." He picked up his briefcase and started to leave.

"Shall I make you a drink?" she called after him. "Vodka martini, isn't it?"

She was either too good to be true or working for that Christmas bonus months in advance. "Uh, that'd be great, thanks," he said, wondering how she'd discovered his cocktail preference. That for sure wasn't on his website. He started to add, "With a twist," then broke off when her voice echoed his. "You psychic or something?" he half joked.

"I wish!" She shot him yet another of those delightfully easy smiles. "But no, I read an article online where you were at some fancy fund-raiser holding a martini and…" Her voice trailed off and she looked down, long lashes sweeping the tops of her very high cheekbones. "I'm acting like a Fan Girl, aren't I? I may as well admit it, I wrote it down in my day planner. I hope you don't mind." She bit on her full bottom lip, a mouth worthy of Angelina Jolie, and Ross felt his throat go dry.

Fan Girl, huh? In her original e-mail, she'd said she liked his show, but he'd been too caught up in assessing her housekeeper potential to give the compliment much thought. "That's very conscientious of you," he said, equal parts flattered and embarrassed.

She gestured with the arm from which his blazer was draped. "I'll just hang this so it doesn't wrinkle, and then I'll bring in your drink." She turned back toward the foyer.

Like sex, it had been a while since someone had tried taking care of him. Not entirely sure how to behave, he started after her. "You don't have to wait on me."

She whipped around, so quickly that they nearly knocked heads. Ross didn't need a mirror to know his ears must be pink. He could feel the telltale burning at the tips. He glanced down at her, but her small smile was about as telling as the Mona Lisa's.

"Gracious, that was close," she exhaled, her free hand

smoothing imaginary wrinkles from her impeccably pressed skirt. "It's no trouble at all. Besides, you're paying me, remember?" Her smile broadened, unearthing a dimple at the side of her chin.

Fixating on that adorable dent, he said, "Well, if you're sure."

Changing course for his study, Ross congratulated himself. It wasn't often that it happened, but so far Martha Jane Gray was exceeding his expectations. The only possible pitfall was *him*. She was so charming and engaging and, okay, pretty, it would be all too easy for him to forget she was an employee and that he'd brought her here first and foremost for Samantha. *Sam.* Sobered, he stepped inside the room, crossed to his desk, and opened up his laptop.

"I made it shaken, not stirred, James Bond style."

Ross nearly jumped out of his skin—his warm, tingling skin. He looked up to find her standing on his threshold, a brimming martini glass suspended in one slender hand.

"That was fast," he said, recovering what composure he had left. He was no James Bond but already he was wondering if Martha Jane wasn't some kind of Wonder Woman.

"I helped put myself through college by waitressing." She crossed to his desk and set the drink down beside the blotter without spilling.

"Impressive," he said, not thinking of the drink. "Self-made men and women are the backbone of this country," he added, both to set her at ease and because he 100 percent meant it.

His folks were working class people, his big brother Ray the first college graduate either side of the family had seen in some time. Both he and Ross had gotten through school with the help of academic scholarships and a patchwork of odd and part-time jobs. Physical labor was hell on the hands but it also built muscle and character. In Ross's opinion, more people should try it. Once he got Sam straightened out to where he no longer felt the need to hover like a hawk, he meant to make sure she got some sort of weekend work; otherwise she'd continue believing that money grew on trees—and that she lived in some kind of eternally enchanted forest.

"Thanks," she said, straightening and taking a step back. "The trick is to keep looking straight ahead, never down. Once you second guess yourself, you're lost."

"Sounds like good advice," he mused aloud. "Maybe you should write a book."

She hesitated, looking suddenly, adorably shy. "Oh, I don't think I'd have a whole big book in me."

"You might be surprised." Adrift in her gray-blue gaze, he reached for the glass, slopping vodka over the rim. Feeling like a klutz, he shook out his wet hand. "As you can see, I'd never make it beyond busboy."

A cocktail napkin materialized in her hand. With brisk efficiency, she wiped up the spillage and stepped back.

He managed to bring the glass to his lips, this time without incident, and took a sip. "This is so good I might think you'd been a bartender."

She laughed, the sound reminding him of the wind chimes on his mother's porch. "Not hardly. I just looked the recipe up online and followed it."

He dropped his gaze to her empty hands. "Aren't you joining me?"

"Well, no, I'm working." She hesitated, and then admitted, "I don't have much of a head for alcohol."

Of course she wasn't about to booze it up. Coming from a small town, she'd probably grown up sipping sweet tea at church socials. It didn't help him that her unspoiled disposition and solid, old school values came packaged in the body of a

Victoria's Secret model.

A buzzer going off drew him back down to Planet Earth.

"That's the oven timer," she said, turning to the door. "Dinner's ready. Why don't you go and make yourself comfortable in the dining room?"

Ross shook his head. "I've never actually seen a single meal come out of that high-end oven. No chance I'm missing out on that." Mrs. Alvarez had left the prepared food in the refrigerator for later reheating.

She bit her bottom lip. "In that case, maybe you could open the wine. I'm afraid I don't have much practice and your corkscrew is a little complicated."

Ross didn't recall his corkscrew as being anything special but, happy to be of use, he said, "You've got it."

He bypassed the breakfast nook and stepped inside the kitchen, fully expecting to be greeted by some degree of culinary chaos. On those rare occasions when his ex had been moved to do more than microwave, their kitchen had resembled the day after an atomic explosion. To his surprise, though, every surface was wiped clean. Not just clean but spotless. The copper pots and pans all hung from their wall hooks and there wasn't so much as a dirty spoon left out.

Salivating, he sniffed the beef-scented air. "Your roast smells amazing."

She smiled. "Let's just hope it tastes amazing as well. It's my mother's recipe with rosemary and pearl onions, and I made parsley buttered potatoes and baby peas to go with it— oh, and biscuits, of course."

He felt his jaw drop. "You baked?"

At her casual nod, he walked over to the oven and opened the door partway. A metal tray of big, fluffy, home-baked biscuits was set inside to warm. Biscuits like his mother made.

"There's dessert, too, but it's a surprise." Her impish grin did funny, fluttery things to his insides.

"That's okay. I like surprises." *I like you*, he was tempted to add, but instead he held out his hands and said, "Put me to work. Where's that wine that needs opening?"

. . .

Ross pushed his chair back from the table and laid a hand on his stomach, which somehow managed the trick of still looking washboard flat despite the heaping plate of food he'd put away. "You keep feeding me like this, and I'm going to have to renew my gym membership."

Macie swallowed a snort. Who did he think he was kidding? A Type A personality like his probably drove him to work out every day at his office gym.

She stuck on a saccharin smile and summoned what her mother might say in such a situation. "After a hard day at work, you deserve to come home to a good meal." To wash the bitter taste from her mouth, she allowed herself a sip of the merlot he'd insisted on pouring her.

The light lines bracketing his mouth relaxed into a smile. She'd seen that smile twice before, the first time on his website and then again at last week's lunch when his daughter had said something that had both exasperated and amused him. But this was the first time it was trained on her, and the full force of it, combined with the focused intensity of those very blue eyes, made her feel as though she'd logged in too many minutes on the tanning bed—disoriented, dry-mouthed, and lightheaded enough to make her glad that she was sitting down.

"You're obviously a young woman who has her priorities in place." Picking up his wineglass, he swirled the ruby liquid around, the picture of male satisfaction.

Could it be this easy? Was simpering submission really what men wanted from a woman? The depressing thought had her casting a longing look at Ross's unfinished martini, wondering if she could get away with siphoning off the final few sips once he left.

"Thank you, Dr. Mannon, I appreciate that, even if there are some who might see it as a sexist statement."

He shrugged as if other people's opinions were the very least of his concern. "I believe men and women are different, fundamentally and biologically. If some people want to call that sexism, let them go right ahead."

She bristled. "So in other words, '*vive la différence*'?"

He nodded approvingly. "The men your age must be fools not to have snapped you up by now. A beautiful, accomplished young woman with your values is hard to come by."

"I suppose I just haven't met the right man yet," she trilled, feeling as if all the oxygen had been vacuumed from the room. Had he really just called her beautiful? Putting off pondering that until later, she glanced pointedly at his plate, which was scraped so clean she could see the cactus pattern at its center, and started up. "If you're finished, I'll just clear these dishes and serve dessert."

To her surprise, he rose as well. "Let me help."

Ross Mannon offering to do dishes? Seriously? "Thanks, but I'll do it. You've worked all day."

"What do you call all this?" He spread his hands, indicating the remains of the roast and the half-empty bowls and platters. "Looks like work to me." His sincere smile had her wishing she'd actually baked those melt-in-your mouth biscuits and peeled a potato or two.

"Okay then, but just set the plates in the sink. I'll put them in the dishwasher later; otherwise you'll spoil the surprise."

"Deal. Only I'll make the coffee, too."

Macie hesitated. "Great, I have the filter ready to go. All you need to do is add two cups of water and hit start."

"I can manage that," he said, following her into the kitchen.

Inside, she grabbed an oven mitt and took out her secret weapon, Stefanie's peach cobbler. Per Stef's instructions, she'd kept the dish warm and loosely covered with aluminum foil. Doing her best to ignore Mannon working at the sink beside her, she set the bubbling pan down on a stove burner and carefully peeled back the foil. Steam rose, the fragrance of sugar-baked peaches filling the kitchen, a mouthwatering olfactory memory from her childhood. Cutting into the thick top crust, she dished up two generous servings into the bowls she'd set out, and then added a scoop of Häagen-Dazs vanilla bean ice cream atop each.

"Hmm," he said, pausing from pouring the brewed coffee into mugs. "Is that—?"

"Peach cobbler," she answered. Bypassing him, she carried the bowls back out to the table. "I hope you like peaches," she said, well knowing he did.

Thoroughly researching one's subject in advance was a cardinal rule of good reporting. A quick Google search on Mannon's family in Texas had brought up a ton of trivia. Apparently his mother's peach pie had taken the Lamar County first-place blue ribbon nearly every year for the past thirty.

He set the coffees down but stayed standing. Holding out her chair, he waited for her to settle in before resuming his own seat. Even knowing what an old school gentleman he was, facing his flawless manners felt…unsettling.

His eyes lit and he answered with a question of his own. "You sure you're not psychic?"

Startled, she dropped her napkin. "Psychic? Why do you

say that?" *God, paranoid much?*

"Ever since I was a kid, I've been partial to anything with peaches—peach ice cream, peach preserves, peach pie, and especially peach cobbler." The grin he gave told her he meant it, that he wasn't just being nice, and she relaxed, for a moment taking genuine pride in having pleased him, an absurdity given her circumstances, as well as dangerous.

Forcing back the feeling, she picked up her fork and punched into the crust. "I would have guessed apple." The sarcasm slipped out unbidden. Shit! She cast a quick glance at Ross's face, searching for signs of fall-out, but his smile held steady.

"Never much cared for baked apples." He dropped his voice and added, "Besides, apple pie started out as British."

She let out a laugh, a real one this time. "'As British as apple pie' doesn't exactly roll off the tongue, does it?"

"No, it doesn't," he admitted, smiling.

Though she despised his politics, really everything he stood for, there was no denying that, one-on-one, Ross Mannon was an exceedingly likeable man.

He turned his attention back to his dessert and forked up a healthy bite. Chewing, he closed his eyes. The sublime look on his face was the kind usually reserved for someone who'd just won the lottery or had incredible sex. Watching him, Macie felt her mouth watering.

He opened his eyes, and she quickly dropped her ogling gaze to her ignored dessert. "This would give my momma a run for her next county fair ribbon, but promise you won't ever let on to her I said so."

Macie heartily doubted she would ever have the occasion to meet Mannon's "momma," but all the same, it was one promise she could honestly make him. "I'll take your confession to the grave."

The next few minutes were silent except for plate scraping. Picking at her portion, Macie used the lull to regroup. She'd had almost two hours solo with her quarry and so far she hadn't gleaned anything of value. Once Sam returned tomorrow, it was hard to say when she'd get him alone again.

He pushed his emptied bowl aside. "I stand by what I said earlier. Someday you're going to make some lucky man a gem of a wife."

She sent him a syrupy smile, thinking he'd just handed her the segue she needed to steer the interview to more intimate terrain. "Thank you, what a nice compliment. Being a wife and mother is my...dearest wish." *Greatest nightmare.* "But first I'm considering going back to school for my Master's," she added, though in reality going anywhere close to a classroom was nowhere in her thoughts.

He nodded and took a sip of coffee. "Education is important and you still have plenty of time for a family."

"I suppose so, but graduate school's such a big commitment, I want to be sure. I saw from your website bio that you were at UNT for almost ten years. If you don't mind my asking, did you take some time off?"

A doctorate in the social sciences typically involved a four-year undergraduate degree followed by a minimum of four years of graduate work; the latter included the requisite classes, master's thesis, doctoral comprehensive exam, and then the grand finale, the doctoral dissertation. Of course many students took longer to finish—from what Macie had seen, grad school was more of a marathon than a sprint—but still, she would have pegged Mannon for one of the few to finish in an even eight.

His facial muscles tensed ever so slightly. A rookie might have missed it, but Macie had been interviewing subjects since her high school newspaper days. "I blew my knee out in the last quarter of the Homecoming game. That pretty much nixed my football career, not to mention my athletic scholarship."

Pressing her advantage, she asked, "Is that when you decided to pursue a career in sociology?"

He laughed and shook his head. "Try road construction."

Road construction, was he putting her on? Then again, maybe he wasn't. She glanced down at his hands, the knuckles shiny with scars.

"You're surprised."

"A little," she admitted, recognizing it wasn't really a question. "It's just that, well, you've become so prominent, a national figure."

He held out his hands and turned them palms up. It wasn't only the tops that had suffered. Thick, raised flesh, the ghost of what must have been some truly wicked calluses, banded the underside of the knuckles. A white scar zigzagged through the right thumb.

"Much of U.S. 271 was repaired with these two hands. I still have the calluses to show for it. To this day I get a kick out of driving and pointing out the stretches I worked on."

Staring down, Macie felt her face flushing. A similar heat pooled in her lower belly. Either the air conditioning had suddenly broken, or the bastard was turning her on.

He dropped his hands under the table. "A good half of the guys on my construction crew were former cons. Some of them became my buddies and later my research subjects. Most were from rural working class church-going families, not all that different from mine. The similarities between us got me curious. What are the drivers that bring a basically good, God-fearing person so low that he'll commit a stupid, in some cases heinous, crime?"

Fascinated, Macie asked, "What did you find?" She'd

meant to at least skim his dissertation but things had moved so quickly she hadn't had time.

"It wasn't income, race, or ethnicity, or whether or not you were a first generation American versus a tenth that made the difference. Having a relative who'd been imprisoned was a minor influencer but the big explanation, the single variable that explained almost forty percent of the behavioral variance, was family structure."

"Family structure?"

He nodded. "It boiled down to whether you'd grown up with two parents at home, or one."

"Let me guess, the children of single parents were more likely to become criminals?' she said, working double time to smooth any edge from her tone.

Expression sober, he nodded again. "Unfortunately, yes. That's why I worry so much about Samantha."

He looked so sincerely, earnestly upset that suddenly it was really hard—impossible—to write him off as just another conservative pig. Still, she couldn't resist adding, "Teenage angst to criminal act seems like a pretty big leap."

He shrugged and blew out a breath. "Maybe or maybe not. Back in New York, Sam shoplifted. It was a crap charm bracelet not worth twenty bucks, and she had more than enough cash on her to pay for it, yet she chose to steal it." His gaze latched onto hers. "Sam shouldn't have to bear the brunt of my screw ups."

The sudden stab of sympathy she felt for him was unwelcome yet irrefutable. "You're being awfully hard on yourself."

Whoa, where had that come from? She'd come here to dismantle the media machine that was Ross Mannon, not to comfort. Bringing the Mighty Mannon low was Operation Cinderella's primary directive. And yet as hard as he was on others, it seemed he was ten times harder on himself. Macie didn't want to, but she couldn't help respecting him for that. More than respect him, she *felt* for him—a dangerous headspace for someone in her position.

He set his jaw. "I've spent the last few years being a more or less absentee father, content with talking to Samantha for our requisite five minutes on the phone every night and getting her for either Thanksgiving or Christmas and one month in the summer. But that's not really parenting, and if I didn't have my own study results to show it, I'd have my gut." He raised desperate, searching eyes to her face, and as much as Macie wanted to look away, somehow she couldn't. "That's the big reason I brought you here, Ms. Gray. Not to cook meals and keep house and run errands, although having those tasks taken care of will be a relief, but because I need help in building a bridge to my daughter. I'm not so sure who she is right now, and I'm pretty sure she feels the same about me. I can't lose my girl, Miss Gray, I just can't."

Macie shook her head. Her throat felt suddenly, suspiciously tight. "You're not going to lose her."

He held out his right hand, a hand that just moments before had seemed the key to unlocking her personal Pandora's Box of fantasies. "With you on my side, Miss Gray, for the first time in weeks, I honestly believe that."

Chapter Five

Francesca's call saying she was in town came as a welcome surprise. Meeting for lunch would be a golden opportunity to catch up and compare notes on Sam, or so Ross figured. Even if they hadn't been coping with a kid in crisis, he would have sincerely looked forward to seeing her. Their divorce was ancient history. Once they'd ceased being warring spouses, they'd fallen back into being friends with fair ease.

The trendy Dupont Circle restaurant wouldn't have been his pick, but as usual Frannie knew her own mind. Also as usual, he was the first to arrive. Taking possession of the table he'd reserved, he flipped open his phone where her text message waited. As he'd expected, she was running late but on her way. He went ahead and ordered their drinks, a glass of pinot grigio for her and a Coors for him. He was halfway through his beer when he spotted her by the hostess stand, a vision of haute couture elegance in a lime suit that caught the color of her almond-shaped eyes. He lifted a hand and flagged her over.

She smiled broadly and made her way toward him through the aisle of tables. "Hullo, darling, sorry to be late.

Traffic was beastly."

Rising, he declined to point out that city traffic was always bad and maybe just once she might try leaving a few minutes early or even on time. Instead he pulled out her chair. "You look good, Frannie."

At thirty-four, Francesca was a sleekly beautiful woman with wavy black hair and jade-colored eyes that turned up slightly at the corners. As a top fashion photographer, her work regularly appeared in *Vogue*, *Elle*, *In Style*, and *Glamour* as well as in a host of European magazines, the names of which he could never remember. Though he wasn't above giving her the occasional hard time over what he saw as the flagrant inconsistency between her liberal political views and voracious materialism, still he was proud of her. Thank God they'd divorced while they were still young enough to mend fences and move on to co-parent their daughter with a minimum of bitterness, a considerable feat for two such drastically different people. She was, without reservation, one of his best friends...so long as he didn't have to be married to her.

She put down her purse, a cavernous caramel-colored shoulder bag so hideous it had to be designer, and slid into her seat. "My, you're looking smashing, not your usual rumpled curmudgeon self at all." She sipped her wine, taking his measure as he sat back down. "New suit, isn't it?" Clothing, Francesca never missed.

He tried for a casual tone. "Yeah, I guess it is."

An earlier impromptu shopping stop to Georgetown Park had started out as a peace offering for Sam. Somehow he'd ended up in Brooks Brothers standing before a display of Italian silk ties and racks of suits.

Eyes alight, Francesca clucked her tongue. "And just when I'd memorized your entire wardrobe, all three dark suits and five striped ties, not counting the army of white button-down Oxfords."

"What can I say, I like keeping you on your toes. How's that wine by the way?"

"Lovely." She took another sip, staring at him over the glass rim. "Though after the week I've had, I could probably use a martini."

"That bad?"

She hesitated, which was unlike her, and finally shrugged. "The shoot in Milan for *Vogue* has been pushed back a week, which means the location bookings, everything will have to be rescheduled. I'm still not entirely certain how I'm to manage it, but of course I will. By the by, I caught your last broadcast."

Her turning the topic away from herself wasn't lost on him, but for now he decided to go with it. "You listened to my show? To what do I owe this honor?"

She picked up her menu and opened it. "One of my prop people happened to mention your name, and I couldn't resist a listen. Mind you, darling, I say this with only love in my heart, but you came off as a perfect pig." She glanced about, feigning concern. "I actually considered coming here in a wig and dark glasses."

He grinned. "Afraid your NOW membership might be revoked if you're caught having lunch with the enemy?" Because he knew it drove her crazy, he continued to ignore the frosted mug their waiter had brought and swigged his beer straight from the bottle.

Wrinkling her nose, she reached over and pulled off the paper cocktail napkin that had stuck to the bottle's bottom. "That would be the very least of it."

He opened his menu and did a quick scan, then glanced to the neighboring table where two ridiculously gargantuan salads had just been served. "Next time I'm picking the restaurant."

"Really, Ross, ingesting one meal of something other than meat and potatoes isn't going to murder you. You've absolutely no appreciation for the culinary arts."

"Funny, I don't remember you being all that culinary when we were married."

Shrugging off his less than subtle reminder of what a disaster she was in the kitchen, she said, "I am, so long as someone else is doing the cooking."

No wonder it hadn't worked out between them. One good thing had come out of their marriage, though, that made even the worst of the pain worthwhile — Sam. Whatever regrets he'd racked up, his daughter wasn't one of them. And then there was the very valuable lesson he'd learned: opposites may attract but they don't stick. When, or rather if, he ever remarried, it would be to a woman who shared his old school values. Until Miss Martha Jane Gray had come along in a swish of soft pastel skirts, he'd given up on such women existing anymore.

He thought of their first night's dinner and a smile lifted his lips. He'd almost forgotten how it felt to sit across the table from another adult and share not just good food but good conversation. Eating alone was no damned fun. Before Sam had moved in, he'd usually grabbed a quick bite on his way home or ordered in Chinese or pizza, which he ate at his desk or in front of the TV while watching the news. But he and Martha Jane must have sat at the table for almost two hours, the coffee growing cold in their cups as they talked about both everything and nothing at all. She was so easy to talk to, to be with. He only hoped he hadn't bored her too badly with his rambling — maybe she'd only been acting interested out of good manners or worse yet, fear of being fired. But neither politeness nor fear came close to explaining how her pretty face had lit when he'd first walked inside the apartment. He couldn't have imagined that—could he?

"Earth to Ross." Francesca's voice pulled him back to the present.

He snapped to, alarmed to realize he'd been blindly staring into space. "Sorry." Hoping he was picking up the last thread of conversation, he asked, "So I take it the boy wonder chef is working out?"

"Frederick isn't a boy. He's coming on twenty-seven. As for the wonder bit, well, you know what they say about an angel in the kitchen and a devil in the bedroom." She winked.

"You can't beat that, I guess."

His thoughts returned to Martha Jane. She obviously had the kitchen part down. Now he found himself wondering where she'd stand on the bedroom half of the equation. She looked so sweet, so adorably innocent that he had a hard time imagining her so much as uncrossing those long, slim legs of hers. And yet there'd been one or two times when he'd been pretty sure he was seeing through to another side of her, one with a dash of the devil in it. Might there be more to her than the sweet, old-fashioned girl that met the eye? That was probably his wishful thinking at work. Several times he'd caught himself mentally peeling off that little print dress and it had taken all his willpower to force his thoughts back to decency. What was going on with him? Sure, he had the normal needs and urges, but having Martha Jane around twenty-four-seven was putting his morality and self-discipline to a grueling test.

Deciding on the sirloin sandwich, one of the few entrees that weren't rabbit food, he snapped his menu closed. He glanced to the wire bread basket and the small brittle bakery items nestled inside. "I don't guess a person could get a regular roll or biscuit around here?" Martha Jane's biscuits had been fluffy as clouds.

Frannie rolled her eyes. "Really Ross, must you be such a Philistine?" She set aside her menu as well. "Along with the food being divine, this is a smashing place to people watch."

"To *beautiful* people watch, you mean. And here I thought you came just to see me."

Now that sparring with Francesca was a novelty and not a day-to-day occupation, he genuinely enjoyed her company. There had even been a handful of times since their divorce when loneliness or plain horniness had brought them precariously close to falling into bed together. Sex was one of the few things they'd done well as a couple. But caring didn't equate to love, at least not the kind he wanted. Fortunately one or both of them had always managed to come back to their senses in time. The friendship they'd rebuilt was too precious to fling away on a whim.

In a quieter voice she said, "We made a beautiful daughter together. We managed to get that part right...or so I thought, until recently."

Ross nodded, his appetite hitting the highway. "Tell me why she ran away, Francesca. I'd just as soon skip the bullshit and have you give it to me straight."

She picked up her wineglass, swirling the amber liquid several times before answering. "She hates her school, she hates New York, and she hates Frederick, but mostly she hates me." Beneath her perfectly cut clothing, her shoulders slumped. She set down her glass and looked pointedly away, but not before he caught the shimmer of tears in her eyes. "I'm famished. Where do you suppose our server's got to?"

"Probably out back stomping more grapes for that high-end vintage you're drinking, so talk to me."

She looked back at him, trying for a smile, but the pooling tears ruined the effect. Ross reached for his handkerchief.

Frannie and he might not see eye-to-eye on a lot of things, but he still understood her. No one could stick a knife in your heart and then twist it deep like your own kid.

She took the hankie from him and used it to blot her eyes. "I'd so hoped we'd divorced before we'd screwed her up too terribly."

He reached across the table and laid his hand atop hers, his only desire to comfort. "Sam's a good kid. She's just going through a rough patch." At least that's what he tried telling himself every damn day. "Besides, all teenage girls hate their mothers. It's practically a rite of passage. If it makes you feel any better, I'm not exactly topping her list of favorite people." He summed up the circumstances leading to his confiscating the magazine.

She sat back in her seat with a sigh. "And yet I spoke to her this morning and she insists she wants to stay on in DC with you...permanently."

Ross withdrew his hand. "Permanently?" That was news to him.

She nodded and sniffed back more tears. "Perhaps she should stay on, for a while at least. You may be a bit heavy handed with discipline, but at least she can count on you to be on the same continent."

Ross froze. "Are you saying she can't count on you for that?"

Her silence was all the answer he needed. Frannie was taking off again. The sinking feeling took him back to that long ago time when she'd handed him a squalling teething toddler and informed him she was taking herself to dinner and a movie before she lost her bloody mind. It was the first time he'd had sole responsibility for Sam. Even though it would only for a handful of hours, the prospect had terrified him. Panicked, he'd called his parents, expecting his mother to bail him out. Instead, she'd informed him she and his dad were having "date night," Sam wouldn't break, and someday he'd look back on the current chaos as "the good old days."

She'd been right on all counts. More than once lately he'd found himself longing for the times when coping with colic, incoming teeth, and skinned knees were his biggest parenting problems.

Frannie waved a hand. "My schedule is madness, as you well know. As I recall, that was one of your chief complaints when we were married, and it's ten times worse now. Depending on where we are in the season, I may have to be in Paris or Milan or Rio at the drop of a hat, often for weeks at a time. That's manageable during the summer when I can take Sam with me or send her to stay with you, but now that she's in high school, I can't withdraw her in the middle of term."

Christ, his own daughter was growing up as a latchkey kid, and until now he hadn't even known it! Outrage flared, and then just as quickly burned inward. What had he thought she'd done with Sam when she went away on location? Stashed her in storage? The uncomfortable truth was that until now he hadn't bothered to think about the details of his daughter's life much at all.

"What she's looking for, whether she understands it or not is stability, and that, Ross, is the very thing I can't give her. But you can…unless, of course, you don't want her."

His spine stiffened. "What the hell is that supposed to mean? She's my kid. Of course I want her." Despite the year of family counseling they'd signed up for after the divorce, Frannie could still push his buttons.

"I'm only saying that if you're in a new relationship, perhaps it isn't the best time to take on a volatile fifteen-year-old living with you."

"As it happens, I'm not in a new relationship and even if

I was, it wouldn't make any damned difference. Sam comes first." Or so she would from here on.

One perfectly plucked brow arched. "You're still alone?"

Apparently it wasn't enough for her to push one or two of his buttons. She had to go for the whole goddamn control panel.

"Sam's staying with me isn't a problem. Let's leave it at that." He picked up his beer, warm now, and finished it off.

She'd turned the tables on him yet again. He might have the PhD, but Francesca was the smart one. Not only had she managed to get him to sign up for sole responsibility of their kid, but now she had him against the ropes defending his love life—or lack thereof.

She took another sip of her wine and studied him. "Oh dear, now I've made you grumpy."

"I am not grumpy." He scanned the floor. Jesus H. Christ, where was their waiter?

She pulled a mock pout. "I know that face of yours. You've all but swallowed your upper lip. You look quite like Ralph Fiennes when you do that. No, don't stop. It's sexy, Ross, really. You'll want to be certain to pull that same face when you're with your new friend."

"She's not my 'new friend' as you put it."

"Ah, so it's an established relationship, even better."

"It's not…I'm not—"

"In a relationship? Well, you're obviously interested in someone. New suit, freshly pressed shirt, and"—she leaned in and sniffed—"cologne."

"Christ, Frannie, lay off. I hired a housekeeper."

She blinked. "Oh my God, you're shagging the housekeeper?"

It was Ross's turn to shush her and look nervously around. "I am certainly not."

She tapped a French-manicured fingernail against her perfectly lacquered lower lip. "Really, Ross, doing the housekeeper is so cliché. Tell me you don't have her dress up in one of those French maid frocks with the fishnets and the silly ruffled caps?"

Ross stared at his empty beer bottle and prayed their server would one day return to bring him another. "I am not…seeing her. We are *not* dating."

"But you fancy her, I can tell. Don't bother to deny it. I know you better than you know yourself, darling, which is why I left you before you could come to your senses and leave me first. But back to the incomparable Miss…"

"Gray."

"Just so, Miss Gray, when do I meet her?"

Never was the response that leaped to mind, but given that Sam would be living with him for the foreseeable future, that wasn't really an option. "Don't you have to be in Milan?"

"Oh darling, that's not until the end of the month. So tell me, where is she from?"

He shrugged. "A small town in Indiana."

Francesca gave a delicate shudder. "I suppose that makes her practically perfect for you."

"Not quite."

"Don't tell me there's trouble in paradise already?" Despite her teasing tone, the little crease furrowing her forehead told him she was genuinely concerned.

Now that she'd wrung a confession out of him, the least she could do was serve as a sounding board. "She's younger."

"Oh dear, this is shaping up to sound like one of those dreadful Gothic romance novels. Sweet young thing becomes housekeeper to brooding lord of the manor."

"Not *that* young. Late twenties…okay, mid-twenties. Twenty-six."

She made a face. "And here you are an old man of thirty-four. But no worries, darling, there's Viagra now, so you and your Miss Gray can look forward to many happy years of fucking."

"Francesca!"

Looking pleased with herself, she clucked her tongue. "Calling me by my full name, you really must be miffed. Do relax, Ross, I couldn't be happier for you and your Miss Gray. Only do try and restrain yourselves in front of our daughter. Mind, I'm supposed to be the kicky, offbeat parent."

"Stop calling her my Miss Gray. She isn't *my* anything. She works for me. If my shirt is pressed, it's because she sent it out to the drycleaner. By the way, you never did say why you're in town."

"Changing the subject, are we? Very well, I'm here for the Heritage Foundation Awards Banquet next week."

Ross nearly spat the mouthful of tap water he'd just taken. "You're going to the Heritage Foundation Banquet?" A social event sponsored by the renowned conservative think tank was hardly Frannie's scene.

She shrugged. "We'll see. Ordinarily I wouldn't consider it, but the theme of this year's dinner is five courses by five regional chefs, and Freddie's been asked to do the foie gras starter. It's quite a coup, really. Only he'll be occupied all night in the kitchen, alas, so I'll be hard-pressed to entertain myself. To be safe, I've finagled a seat at one of the VIP tables alongside you, Mr. Republican of the Year!"

So she knew about his award. He sat back, folding his arms over his chest. "Great, you'll have to tell me how it went."

"You're not going?" She shook her head in apparent despair. "But you must, you're receiving a no-doubt-coveted award!" Dropping her voice, she asked, "Is it because you... can't get a date?"

He bristled. "Who says I can't get a date?"

"Mind you, showing up dateless to a black tie affair in DC is the surest way to convince people you're gay."

"That's ridiculous."

"I'm warning you, Ross, if I must I'll engage an escort on your behalf."

He wouldn't put it past her. The very last thing he needed was to show up on some DC madam's roster as another Client Number Nine.

To get her off his back, he blurted out, "Okay, I'll go—with a date and *without* your help, thank you very much. In fact, I have…someone already in mind."

• • •

Ross's lunch appointment provided Macie with the perfect opportunity to sneak Stefanie in for a tour of the apartment as well as a food drop off. Going room-to-room and seeing her friend's awed reaction brought an absurd sense of pride. Several times Macie had to remind herself that the apartment she was showing wasn't actually her home.

Looking around, Stef said, "Wow, this is some place. I always wondered what the Watergate apartments were like. Until now, I'd only been to the restaurant." Backtracking to the kitchen, she unzipped the last of the insulated food-carrying bags she'd brought for that night's dinner. "So, how'd your first night go?"

Caught in a web of conflicting feelings, Macie took a moment to answer. "It went fine, thanks."

Stef stopped in mid-zip. "Just fine?" She sounded a little deflated.

"I mean, it went really well. He was bat shit for the food. Your biscuits were a big hit. He had three, called them slices of heaven because they were light and fluffy as clouds."

Stef beamed. "I don't care what his politics are, the man has taste."

Stefanie's mom, Rosaria, had taught her to cook at a very young age, so young she'd started out standing on a stool to reach the countertop. These days she had a growing roster of clients who appreciated her culinary efforts and were willing to pay top dollar. Still, if Macie could make one wish come true for her friend it was that Stefanie might meet a man who appreciated all she had to offer, including but not limited to mouthwatering meals. So far, no luck. It didn't help that Stef was self-conscious about her weight. Listening to her so-called jokes about her cottage cheese thighs and bubba butt made Macie's heart hurt. If only she'd ditch the baggy sweaters, oversized T-shirts, and elastic waist jeans for clothes that complemented her curves rather than camouflaged them, she'd shine as a knock-out, Macie was sure of it.

Then again, it wasn't like being a fashion diva had done Macie much good. All the La Perla lingerie and Jimmy Choo shoes in her closet hadn't kept Zach from cutting out on her repeatedly. Sure, she dated a bunch, but it was Manhattan. Everybody did. Other than Zach, most of her dates never got beyond the third meet-up. Barring a haphazard handful of hot moments, she spent almost as much time solo as Stef did. Macie imagined the stacked take-out and microwaveable meal-for-one boxes she'd amassed over the last five years might reach to the moon.

"So what's he like?" Stef's question startled her back to the present.

Walking her fingers along the granite countertop, Macie shrugged. "He's okay, I guess."

Ross was, she admitted—albeit to herself—better than okay, unfailingly courteous and kind and even funny, altogether at odds with his starchy public persona. Even after just one night, she was starting to wonder if his clean living act might not be an act at all. After dinner, he'd given her his calendar for the month and from what she saw, other than one banquet, a political thing, he didn't plan to socialize—no happy hours, let alone any adult "sleepovers," none that she could tell, anyway. Aside from taking early morning runs along the Potomac, he seemed determined to devote whatever free time he could find to Sam.

Stefanie spoke up. "You know, Mace, traditional values aren't all bad. Back when my mom was still alive, it was nice being part of a family where you knew you could count on everybody to have your back, and they knew they could count on you."

Assuming they really have your back, Macie mentally added, thinking of her own parents and how they'd fundamentally failed her. For whatever reason, she found herself admitting, "One-on-one, he's actually kind of...sweet and easy to talk to."

She'd exchanged more substantive words in one dinner with Mannon than she had with Zach in three years. But then she was starting to see that she and her ex hadn't had a relationship, not really. All that time they'd been, as Zach put it, just "hanging out."

Shaking off the sadness that epiphany brought, she added, "After dinner, he insisted on helping me clean up. Thank God I'd taken the kitchen trash out to the compactor before he got home, otherwise he would have spotted the catering boxes and then my goose would have been cooked. Speaking of which, what's cooking for tonight?"

"I made spaghetti and meatballs. Don't worry, I made Samantha's with texturized soy protein and put it in a separate container. See, I marked them as mock balls so you can keep them separate." Stef lifted the plastic container with the pink Post-it.

Macie blew out a breath. "Thanks, you've probably saved me from having her pitch the saucepot over my head."

"The *real* meatballs are made with ricotta and...well, you may be my best friend, but I don't know that I can bring myself to give up my secret ingredient even to you."

"Suit yourself. But either way your secret's safe with me. Stealing your ingredients would only lead to cooking and you know when it comes to the kitchen my mantra's always been 'Just Say No.'"

Stephanie finished re-sealing the bags. "Cooking can be a lot of fun when you have someone like my pop who appreciates good food and the time and care that goes into preparing it. From what you've said, it sounds like Ross Mannon might be that kind of guy."

Macie wasn't sure what to say to that, so for once she said nothing. Stef studied her. "You know Mace, other than my biscuits and baklava, there's not much in life that's one hundred percent perfect, including people."

Sensing she might be on the receiving end of a lecture, Macie bristled. "Your point is?"

Stef shrugged. "Just consider it...food for thought."

•

Stef had been gone all of five minutes when stomping footsteps announced that Samantha Mannon was home early from her school trip to The White House. Talk about a close call.

Coming into the kitchen, she announced, "Something smells good."

Considering this wasn't only an olive branch but a whole

olive tree, Macie resolved to make an effort. "Thanks, I made my famous spaghetti sauce and meatballs."

"Famous, huh? You mean like you made all the stuff from scratch?"

Obviously the kid was impressed—as well she should be. Macie nodded. "I've been peeling tomatoes all morning."

"You sure are industrious, Miss Gray." She pressed her foot down on the trash can pedal. The lid popped up, and she leaned over to look inside.

Macie's heart slammed to a stop. She hadn't had the chance to carry the trash to the compactor. The liner brimmed with boxes and discarded packaging emblazoned with the Good Enuf to Eat name and logo, hallmarks of professional catering in plain...*evidence.*

"Samantha, don't touch that!"

Startled, Sam jumped back and the stainless steel lid slammed closed. Had she seen inside?

Macie searched the girl's face, but it was as blank as a professional poker player's. "Jes—*jiminy*, you should wash your hands. Garbage containers carry all kinds of germs."

Gaze riveted on the can, Samantha made no move toward the sink. "We're learning about composting in Biology class. Did you know some people keep worms to feed their leftovers to and then the worms—well, you're going to love this part—crap it all out and then they use the poop for—"

"Fertilizer, yes I know." Was the kid out to torture or bore her to death?

"I was thinking of doing that for my science fair project. Maybe you could start saving the scraps from all the great meals you're making us."

Macie scraped a hand through her hair. *Christ, I could seriously use a cocktail.* "I don't know, I'll think about it."

Stuffing her hands in her jeans' pockets, Sam took a long

look around. "Where are all the dirty pots?"

Perspiration beading her brow, Macie snapped, "I already washed them, why?"

Sam shot a look to the wall rack from which the cluster of copperware hung, shiny as mirrors. "My grandma in Texas makes her spaghetti sauce in a big stew pot, and she lets it simmer for the whole day. It gives her hours and hours to work on the pasta—with the pasta maker." She looked pointedly at the counter. Other than the microwave, toaster, and Mannon's much-used coffeepot, there were no other appliances out.

Macie propped her fisted hands on her hips. "I guess I use a shorter recipe."

"Maybe you could let me have it so I can e-mail it to Grandma, save her some time, seeing as how she's in her golden years and all."

The kid was Satan's spawn, no doubt about it. "Don't you have some homework to do?"

"Some reading for English Lit," Sam admitted. "That Jane Eyre sure steps into some serious shit." Smirking, she turned and sauntered out.

Watching her go, Macie let out the breath she'd been holding. Was Sam onto her? If so, then the kid's game, Macie surmised, would be to hold the threat over her head for as long as she could and then produce her trump card when it really counted. At least that's how Macie would play it were their positions reversed. Hopefully by then she'd have enough on Mannon to make her exit, and nothing else would matter. All the more reason to get on the J.O.B.

She left the kitchen and tiptoed past Sam's closed bedroom door. A conversation in progress confirmed the kid was within, either talking on her cell or video chatting—so much for *Jane Eyre*. Mannon's study lay at the far end of the hallway. She stepped inside, closing the door softly behind her. He'd left his laptop lying open on his desk—talk about trusting. It was apparently password unprotected and still running. He must have dashed out that morning without logging off. Keeping one eye on the study door, she leaned over the desk and began scrolling through his history of recently visited sites.

Holy shit! Macie blinked, at first disbelieving her eyes. Talk about hitting pay *dirt*. Links to "erotica" chat rooms, sketchy "costuming" sites, and yes, seriously raunchy porn greeted her. She spotted what was obviously a kiddie porn site among the list and anger bubbled up inside her. Playing with adults was one thing, but getting your kicks from kids was beyond sick. Hands shaking, she took a screen shot, logged off and back on again as a guest, and e-mailed it to herself, then deleted the copy from the Sent folder.

Queasy, she stepped away from the desk. What the hell was wrong with her? She'd just been handed the equivalent of Mannon's severed head on a platter and the best she could do was pray she didn't puke. She should feel relieved, vindicated, triumphant, but instead what she felt was absurdly, irrationally let down. More than let down, she felt crushed, as though she'd just found out Santa Claus was a myth and the tooth fairy just another fake. She'd been halfway to believing that, politics aside, Ross Mannon might be an actually decent guy, but now she saw she'd been right about him from the beginning. On the surface he might look like a prince but beneath that patina of man pretty was a warty frog waiting to leap free. Worse, he was the scum on the bottom of the pond where the other frogs lived—so much for friggin' fairy tales.

She straightened her shoulders and willed her stomach to calm. It was time to stop acting like a rookie and start being the professional she'd worked so hard to become. The full story remained to be flushed out, but in the interim, this update on Ross's Internet trolling should satisfy Starr that she really was on to something big.

Back in her room, she forwarded the screenshot to Starr with a cc: to Terri. She'd just dropped her phone in the bottom of a dresser drawer when she heard stirring in the foyer — Ross, of course. The sick son-of-a-bitch was home early and likely eager to log in some more perverted private playtime with his laptop. Macie stood, sucked down a deep breath, and reached for her game face. She drew the door closed behind her and stepped out, the plush hallway carpet seeming to suck at her soles, and her body trembling. Why did this suddenly feel so...*hard*?

"Did you have a nice day?" she asked, coming out into the main room.

"I did." He turned away from the coat rack to face her and she spotted it at once — a smear of classically dark red lipstick on his jaw.

More confirmation of his scumbag status! When it rained dirt, it apparently poured it as well.

Feeling as though an entire bacco bed were being dumped onto her head, she forced herself to take a step closer. "You have lipstick on your cheek."

He turned to the wall mirror, tilted his face, and blushed. "Sheesh, Frannie could have said something." He dug inside his pocket, came up empty, and settled for scrubbing at the spot with the back of his hand.

Frannie? Given his packed schedule, "Frannie" was either the most understanding girlfriend on the planet or one who got paid by the hour. Macie would put her money on the latter.

Apparently catching her questioning look, he supplied, "Sam's mother showed up in town at the last minute, and we took the opportunity to have a parental powwow over lunch."

"Your lunch was with Sam's...mother?" Focusing on the lipstick leavings, she added, "It's nice that you've stayed so... friendly."

Turning away from the mirror, he grimaced. "Having a kid in common is a powerful motivator to play nice."

A laudable sentiment—or at least Macie would have thought so if she hadn't just seen his Internet history. Even if he had just come from a platonic lunch with his ex, he was still a serious sicko. She couldn't afford to lose sight of who and what he was—and what she'd come to DC to do. At this rate, she'd be back in New York long before her allotted six weeks.

Operation Cinderella was moving ahead at full throttle.

Chapter Six

The next morning, all hell broke loose. Carrying his open laptop into the kitchen, Ross wore a face reddened with fury and his tie loose about his neck. Macie tensed. Had he found out about her snooping? Had Sam revealed her suspicions so soon? She glanced over to the kid, expecting to see a smirk, but for once Sam seemed to have nothing sarcastic or otherwise to say. Picking poppy seeds off a bagel, she hunkered on one of the counter stools, head down and mouth shut.

"Dr. Mannon, whatever is the matter?" Macie asked, not entirely successful at smoothing the tremor from her tone.

He slammed the laptop atop the breakfast bar, rattling the glasses of orange juice she'd just poured. "See for yourself."

The screen showed the *On Top* blog with the header for that day's post, "Perverse Pleasures? Conservative Media Pundit, Ross Mannon, Addicted to…'Love'?"

"The station's PR people run a daily Google Alert to track media hits," he explained, raking a hand through his shower-damp hair. "The search engine brought up this…crap. Apparently late yesterday, an 'anonymous reader' broke the story on my supposed Internet pornography addiction." He shook his head, color still high. "The sites they list turn my stomach."

Staring at the screen, Macie felt almost as stunned as he did. Apparently Starr had taken her "interim report" and published it as fact.

"I'm sorry," she said, surprised that she actually was.

Out of the corner of her eye, she glimpsed Sam, face paling. Then again what kid, no matter how tough talking, wouldn't be devastated to discover that her dad was a porn addict? Thanks to Macie, she just had.

Turning her gaze back on Mannon, she asked, "What are you going to do?"

"The station's legal department's already on it. We'll demand a retraction—and an apology."

Feeling weak in the knees, she braced a hand against the counter. "And if you don't, um…get it?"

"We'll sue." He closed the laptop without turning it off. "Hopefully the station will get behind me on this, it's in my contract, but if I have to I'll take on the sons-of-bitches myself." He looked over to Sam. "I don't want you to worry about any of this, honey. It's all a load of—a big mistake, but I'm working on fixing it. Okay?"

Sam swallowed, looking like she might be sick. "O… okay," she echoed, her voice unlike Macie had ever heard it, weak and trembling like…like a child's.

He dropped a kiss atop Sam's head. "I'm going into the office. I'll see you ladies later." He picked up the laptop and left.

The front door opening then closing confirmed he'd gone. Sinking onto the stool beside Sam, Macie looked down at the platter of bagels that no one, including her, seemed to want to eat. "Sam, are you going to finish that bagel or do you want to take it with you in the car? If we don't leave in the next five, you'll be late for school."

Sam dropped the bagel she'd still held. "I don't feel so good."

Macie stood. "Nice try, but I'm not buying. Get your backpack and let's go. Your dad has enough on his mind without getting a call from your school." *Thanks to me*, she silently added.

Sam stayed put. "I'm not faking, I swear."

The kid's stricken face told her she was telling the truth. "Sam, I know you're upset, and I don't blame you, but your dad said he would fix this and...and I'm sure he will."

"It's my fault." Sam planted her elbows on the counter and buried her head in her open hands. "Dad's going to kill me or at least hate me forever."

Staring down on the kid's bowed head, Macie reached for her patience. Fifteen was a tough age under the best of circumstances. Whatever was wrong in Sam's world might not be any big deal, but right now it obviously seemed pretty big to Sam.

"Your father could never hate you, not forever, not even for five minutes. He loves you too much, but you'd better tell me what you did."

Sam lifted her head from her hands. Her cheeks were wet and her eyes ran with fat tears. "Dad didn't visit those websites. I did."

The shock hit, not so much a full on strike as a face slap, a wakeup call. Stronger still was the relief, so strong it skirted the edges of what felt, suspiciously, like Macie remembered joy had once felt. Mannon didn't surf for porn, not kiddie porn, not adult porn, either. He wasn't a pervert. He wasn't a fiend. Whatever his deep, dark secret might or might not be, it wasn't *that*.

Thoughts racing, she listened to the rest of Sam's tearful

confession, simultaneously stringing together the details and strategizing what might be done to limit the damage. Pissed off that her dad had implemented the parental control function on her computer and inspired by the Declaration of Independence, which she was studying in her American History class, Sam had decided to stage her own mini revolt. She'd snuck into Ross's study, found his login and password written on a Post-it note stuck to the inside of his unlocked desk drawer, and used his laptop to log onto the skankiest sites she could find. Not to get him into any trouble—she'd never seen that coming—but to prove that he couldn't restrict her access and deny her "liberty." The kid was considerably fuzzier on the nature of the exact object lesson she'd meant to impart, but Macie surmised it had to do with wanting to show that she was an adult as well as equal in the smarts department. That didn't make logical sense, of course, but being a rebel herself, as well as her own worst enemy, Macie got it.

Plaintive eyes latched onto hers. "What am I gonna do?"

It was the first time Sam had asked for her help or even her opinion. Having her do so now warmed Macie to the tips of her toes. It also scared her shitless. Acting as someone else's moral compass put her definitely out of her element, far out. And yet here she was with the poor kid literally looking up to her, casting her sad, hopeful gaze on Macie, waiting for her answer as though she were the Dalai Lama.

She reached over and laid her hand on the kid's cold one. "The way I see it, there's only one thing you can do." She drew a deep breath, bracing herself to deliver the message that no child under any circumstances ever wanted to hear. "You're going to have to come clean and tell your dad the truth."

Predictably, Sam's eyes bugged. "Tell him I'm the one who's made the whole world think he's a perv? He'll *kill* me."

Feeling like the biggest hypocrite on the planet, Macie squeezed her hand. "You don't have to tell him alone. If you want, I'll be there standing beside you. We'll tell him together."

Sam sniffed into her fisted free hand. "Really?"

"Yes, really. Now go grab your book bag so you're not late."

Other than the car radio, the drive to Bethesda was made in silence. Driving Mannon's Ford Explorer down commuter-clogged Wisconsin Avenue, catching nearly every red light, Macie mentally calculated the damage already done. If a Google Alert had picked up the post, it had likely already gone viral. She had to call Starr and set her straight.

What about "interim update, extremely confidential" hadn't been clear? More to the point, what had possessed her to send that e-mail so quickly? As a professional, the very first thing she should have done was to ask herself who besides Mannon had access to his computer. She should have dug deeper, ruled out every other possible person, before releasing her findings as fact. She should have…

The sign for Sidwell Friends was before them. She put on her turn signal and pulled into the school's drop off lot. For more than 125 years, the nation's finest minds had been formed on this campus of weathered stone and sprawling lawns. Sam, whether she knew it or not, was being groomed to take her place among them. Macie might be in the girl's life for just six weeks, but she was suddenly struck with the gravitas of the charge she'd been given.

Glum-faced, Sam opened the car door and got out.

Impatient as she was to make her call, still Macie beckoned her back. "Sam?"

Backpack slung over one shoulder, Sam turned around. "Yeah?"

"It's going to be okay—really."

"Yeah, right, for you maybe. Once Dad kills me, you two can dump my body in the Potomac. With all the pollution, I'll probably dissolve."

Macie sighed. So much for a definitive détente. "It's a good suggestion, thanks. I'll pass it on to your father after I've finished sharpening the kitchen knives."

"Or maybe an acid bath like in *Pulp Fiction*," Sam added with a smirk.

Despite the dire situation they were all in, Macie found herself holding in a chuckle. Mannon's kid was a character all right. Not many people would appreciate Sam's morbid sense of humor, but Macie was starting to.

"I'll consider it. For now, off to school, Morticia."

Sam closed the car door, but not before Macie spotted her small smile. Feeling fractionally better herself, she reached for her BlackBerry.

Starr answered her cell on the third ring. "What's up, Cinderella?"

"You tell me," Macie said. "I send you an interim update and you explode the story, *my* story, without me?"

"Upset I let Terri have the byline, huh?"

Teeth gritted, Macie answered, "It's not about that. That e-mail was meant as an update only. It turns out Mannon didn't visit those websites. His…someone else with access to his computer did." Mentioning Samantha might make things even worse.

Starr's snort struck Macie in the ear like a spitball. "Yeah, right, and I'm Mother Goose. Are you sure you're not starting to take this fairy-tale metaphor a little too seriously?" When Macie didn't respond, she added, "Look, I made a strategic decision, one that will, in all likelihood, build buzz for your exposé. In the meantime, we'll hopefully also generate enough interest to ramp up sales so we recoup our lost ad monies. In a word, *winning*!"

It was hard but Macie let her finish. "So, it's all about the bottom line." So much for Upton Sinclair, so much for seeing herself as a serious journalist. She was nothing more than a revenue generator, not so very different from the sales reps who sold the actual ads.

A sigh sounded. "Don't tell me it's taken you five years to get that, but yes, Macie, we're in the magazine *business*. Not a charity but a business. Next time, don't send me something you haven't one hundred percent checked out."

Gripping the steering wheel with her free hand, Macie firmed her voice. "You need to know that this time Mannon's not going to be satisfied with attacking us verbally to his listeners. If you don't take down that post and issue a retraction, he's going to sue."

Starr scoffed. "Let him bring it on."

Macie knew her boss better than to expect an apology, but this callous disregard for the truth, and the consequences of continuing to support a lie, stunned her. "He won't be alone. The network has deep pockets and his contract ensures they'll use every last dollar to fight to clear his name—not to mention sue for damages." The latter might be true. It might also be a bluff. Whichever—she only hoped it would work.

Starr hesitated. "I'll have the IT people take down the post. As for the retraction, I make no promises."

"But I just told you—"

"Did those sites show up in his web history or did they not?'

"Yes, but I know for a fact that he didn't visit them. It was someone else. Okay, it was his kid. She did it as a prank."

"And you know this how?"

Macie hesitated. "She told me."

"Has it not occurred to you she might be lying to cover

for her old man?'

"She's not like that."

Starr scoffed again. "You've been there what, a few days, and already you're an expert on their family dynamics? Are you a psychologist or a reporter, Graham?"

The question didn't merit a response, but Macie gave one anyway. "I'm a reporter."

"Great, then bring me a story the public can sink its teeth into. I want it real, and I want it big."

Starr ended the call before Macie could answer. It was just as well. What more was there for her to say?

It was a good thing she'd decided against driving and not only because she didn't have her hands-free device and earbuds with her. She laid a clammy palm on the cool steering wheel and focused on calming her racing heart. She'd first come to New York to be a serious journalist. The same desire had brought her back to DC, yet suddenly and in so many ways she felt a long way from "home." Worse, she didn't know what "home" meant anymore.

By noon, the blog post had been taken down, albeit without apology or explanation. That was something, Macie supposed, if not exactly enough. Predictably a few regional liberal media outlets had latched onto the story but as far as she knew it had slipped beneath the radar of the national news—at least so far. She only hoped Ross's PR people were sufficiently savvy in reputation management to have begun burying the story.

Evening rolled around. As usual, Stef had outdone herself—oven-baked barbecue breast of chicken, rice pilaf, and cilantro pineapple salsa for the carnivores and tofu sliders with rosemary-and-sea-salt-dusted fries for Sam—still, everyone picked at their food.

It took several aborted attempts, but finally Sam got the

sentence out. "Dad, I have something to tell you."

Ross looked up from the pineapple square he'd been pushing around his plate. "What is it, honey?"

Macie reached across and took Sam's hand. "Go ahead."

Looking between them, Ross said, "Now you've got me worried."

Squeezing her hand hard, Sam drew a shaky breath and started spilling her story. Predictably, Ross was at first shocked and finally steaming mad.

"In sneaking to those sites, you put my computer's IP address out there to be captured by everyone and anyone. The son-of-a-bitch who reported me probably also hacked into my computer, and now my career and reputation are on the line. I've been in consultation with the attorney for damned near half the day. Do you even realize how many hours of people's time and thousands of dollars have been *wasted*? No, of course you don't. Well, you'll have lots of time to think about it because you, young lady, are grounded. You go to school and back and that's it."

Sam released Macie's hand at last. Now that she was neither cast out nor killed, she looked like she might dissolve into a puddle at any time.

Flexing numbed fingers, Macie looked to Sam and said, "I think we can work with that, can't we, Sam?"

"Yeah, I guess so." Mouth trembling, she asked, "For how long?"

"For as long as I say," Ross snapped. "Now come here. Come *here*."

Slowly she got up from her place and rounded the table. Stopping in front of him, she lifted wary eyes to his. "I'm too old for a spanking, right?"

He released a weary breath. "I don't know about you, but I surely am. And I know we could both use this." He opened his arms—and enfolded his daughter in a seriously huge hug.

Samantha sobbed into his chest. "Oh, Daddy, I'm so sorry."

Patting her back, he said, "I know you are, honey."

Looking on, Macie felt as if her heart were squeezing in on itself. Whatever else Ross Mannon was—conservative talking head, sexist pig, the man who might yet get her fired—he was also a really good father. And he deserved to hear it.

She waited until Samantha went to her room before saying, "You're an awesome dad."

He grimaced. "Thank you, that's nice to hear. Especially when a healthy portion of the American public will probably end the week thinking I'm a pedophile."

"I mean it. Sam's lucky to have you. After today, I think she realizes that, too."

Leaning back in his chair, he stared at her for an unnervingly long time. Finally he said, "How do you do it, Miss Gray?"

"Sir?"

"How do you manage to make me feel better in the midst of one of my blackest moments?"

Embarrassed by receiving praise she so clearly didn't deserve, Macie got up to clear the table.

"No, leave it." Mannon waved her back into her seat. "Talking to you is a hell of a lot better than any therapy."

Warmed, still she forced herself to remember that she had dirt to find—and a story to write. "What would you know about being in therapy?"

The second the words were out, she felt her face flame. Open mouth, insert foot much? He'd already revealed to her that Sam was seeing a psychologist. Christ, he'd even included the weekly "doctor's" appointment in the schedule he'd given her.

"That was tactless of me. I am so sorry." Crazy as it might be, she really was.

He shrugged. "Actually Sam's mom and I logged in some time in family counseling after the divorce, trying to work through our 'anger issues' as the therapist called them, so we could co-parent Sam."

Remembering the lipstick smudge, she said, "I guess therapy worked."

He hesitated. "It helped some but what helped more than anything was the two of us talking one-on-one. Late one night when we were both really stressed out and fed up, we called a truce, sat down over a pot of coffee for me and tea for her, and made a pact. No matter how many hours it took or how tired or pissed off either one of us felt, we didn't get to leave until we'd fixed things to the point where we could be good parents to Sam."

"That's really inspiring." It was.

"I thought we had a pretty smooth sailing arrangement until Sam showed up here in the middle of the night. I'd started to lose hope—and then you came to us. I know you haven't even been here a full week, and yet already I'm beginning to wonder how we ever got along without you." The warm look he sent had her heart turning over—and her guilt ratcheting.

Speaking over the lump lodging in her throat, she said, "I'm just the housekeeper. I don't do anything special." *Other than working double time to ruin your life...*

But Mannon was adamant. "That's where you're wrong, Miss Gray. Everything you do is special."

• • •

The awards dinner was on Saturday, just three days away. Almost a week had passed, and Ross had yet to ask Martha

Jane to go. Sure, he'd been busier than a one-armed bandit, staying late at the station and putting out the last of the fires over that damned blog, but if he were honest with himself, it wasn't time he lacked. It was courage.

Drumming his fingers on the kitchen countertop one evening in the wake of yet another mouth-watering meal, he wondered what the hell he was afraid of. He was Ross Mannon, the same Ross Mannon whose voice and opinions found their way inside tens of thousands of American households every week. So, why was he suddenly acting—and feeling—like a sweaty-palmed high school kid about to ask out the prom queen?

"Miss Gray, you have a minute?"

Martha Jane closed the cupboard on the coffee cup she'd just put away and turned to him, piercing him with her blue-gray gaze. How did women do it, stand there looking so serene and cucumber cool when the man was sweating bullets into his shirt collar?

"Certainly, what can I do for you?" she asked.

Talk about your loaded question.

He hesitated. His hands hadn't been this sweaty since he'd first struck up the nerve to touch a girlfriend's breast. "I have something to ask you, a favor really. First, though, I want you to know it's perfectly okay for you to say no."

She sent him a gentle smile. "Maybe you should just tell me what it is?"

"I have this…thing coming up on Saturday night, an awards banquet and well, it's not really the kind of event you go to alone. Not that I *can't* go by myself—I can—it's just that I was wondering—"

"Dr. Mannon, are you by chance asking me to go with you?"

"I guess I am. But look, if I'm out of bounds here, you

just say the word and I'll back off. I don't want to make you uncomfortable." Asking out his housekeeper, his hot, young housekeeper…if there was ever a textbook setup for a sexual harassment suit, this had to be it.

As if reading his mind, she said, "Easy, professor, I'm not about to hit you with a sexual harassment suit if that's what you're worried about. And yes, I'd love to go."

The relief rushing him was beyond reason. Until now, he hadn't realized how much he'd been dreading going dateless.

"That's terrific. Only I don't know how much fun you'll find it. It's one of those stuffy formal affairs, an awards program with speakers. We'll be sharing a table with six others, so it's not like you'll be stuck with just me."

She looked amused. "Thanks, but I wasn't worried. I assume it's black tie?"

"Yes," he admitted, feeling so much like his former pimply-faced teen self that it took a conscious effort to keep from shuffling his feet. "I hope that doesn't present a problem." He paused, thinking he should probably offer to pay for a dress but at a loss as to how to offer without offending her—or embarrassing them both.

She saved him with a single headshake. "I'll pull something together."

"Thanks, you're saving my life here. We don't have to stay all that long, just until the awards are handed out."

"If you don't mind my asking, why are you going if you dislike it so much?"

"Because, I'm uh…" He hesitated, feeling sweat break out on his forehead. "I'm receiving one of the awards."

Her eyes widened. "Wow, congratulations. May I ask in what category?" He hesitated and she let out a light laugh. "If you'd rather, I can wait and read it in the program."

"Republican of the Year," he admitted, feeling shy—

make that mortified. His work life was one thing, but socially he'd always been more of an introvert.

"That's quite an...honor."

He shrugged, feeling his ears heat. "Ordinarily I would skip it and let them send me the trophy or plaque or whatever the hell...heck it is by mail. But in light of the situation with the blog post, the network is pretty insistent that I go. Considering the money and man hours Sam's escapade has cost, I can't very well bail."

"I see."

"It won't really be a date. You'll be my dinner companion. And of course I'll compensate you for your time."

Her smile thinned. "You want to *pay* me to go out with you?" The color flooding her face confirmed he'd stepped into a pile of it. "Please understand, Dr. Mannon, I'm happy to be your dinner companion for the evening, but I wouldn't dream of billing you for my time." He started to protest, but she silenced him with a look. The only other woman who'd ever pulled that off was his mom. "It's not every day that a girl from Heavenly, Indiana, gets to rub elbows with Washington's power elite. Really, it's you who'll be doing me the favor, giving me the chance to play Cinderella for a night."

Ross hadn't quite looked at it like that. "Well, if you're sure I won't be imposing."

"Not a bit. I can hardly wait to tell the folks back home."

• • •

The first of the "folks" Macie called was Franc. Cuddled up under her comforter several hours later, she whispered into her cell phone, "It looks like Maddie's shoes will be getting a test drive after all. I'm going to a ball, or at least to a banquet, on Saturday."

"That's great, love, who with?"

It was a natural question. People didn't typically attend banquets without a plus one. Still, she took a moment before admitting, "Ross Mannon."

She thought back to his earlier shyness, which she'd found refreshing, endearingly so. Then again maybe playing shy was his M.O. and hitting on the help his secret weakness. Samantha had mentioned someone named Mrs. Alvarez. Visions of a Jennifer Lopez lookalike flashed through Macie's mind and inexplicably she felt...jealous. She made a mental note to look up Ross's former housekeeper, maybe have a chat with her, assuming she was still in the area.

Franc sighed. "I've seen his photos. He's yummy."

"I know how you love to match make, but this is *work*," Macie insisted, wondering which of them she was trying hardest to convince. "I'm on assignment, remember? This dinner will be my first chance to observe him in the field among his peers."

Franc chuckled. "Whatevs, Margaret Meade. Fill me in on the deets starting with what you're wearing."

"Good question," she admitted. "Other than your shoes, I didn't pack anything formal."

"Sounds like little Miss Cinderella needs to take herself shopping," he said.

"I'm going first thing tomorrow."

Fortunately The Shops at Georgetown Park were a short drive away. Housed in a former nineteenth century tobacco warehouse in the tony Georgetown historic district, the upscale mall was certain to deliver on a banquet-worthy dress. Whatever she got, it would have to be killer, striking the perfect balance between subtle and sexy.

Because although Saturday night might not be a date in the true sense of the word, a part of her wanted Ross Mannon to wish it was.

· · ·

Saturday night rolled around before Ross knew it. He'd delayed putting on his monkey suit—tuxedo—until the last possible minute, yet still he was the first one ready. Macie had disappeared into her room a little over an hour ago and had yet to surface. But he didn't mind waiting. Black-tie affairs weren't his thing, and award or not, he wasn't in any rush to get to this one. Besides, hanging out gave him the opportunity to log in one-on-one time with Sam. Even though she was grounded, he wanted to make sure she didn't feel shunned. Unlike the Internet, TV was still on the menu of sanctioned pleasures. He settled next to her on the sectional sofa to watch the movie she'd already started.

Caught up in *Back to the Future*, he lost temporary track of time. A soft, manufactured cough carried him back to the present. He looked back over his shoulder—and felt the breath rush from his lungs.

Martha Jane stood on the living room threshold wearing a little black cocktail dress and not much else. The hemline didn't exactly qualify as a mini, but it hit above the knee. A twinkle caught his eye. Almost against his will, he followed the beacon downward, his gaze skimming long, shapely legs and trim ankles to slender feet shod in red high-heels beaded with brilliants.

Ross leaped up, the remote slipping from his suddenly nerveless fingers. "You look…"

Wow came to mind, but he reminded himself that mature, mid-thirties men didn't use words like that, at least not anymore. He drove his gaze back up to her face, doing his damnedest to bypass the swell of bosom set off by her dress's modest scooped neckline, and confirmed it wasn't only the shoes that sparkled. Her gaze meeting his had him thinking of sapphires.

"You look really hot," Sam said for him, pulling her gaze from the TV and giving Martha Jane the once-over.

Martha Jane let out a nervous laugh. "Thanks, Sam, that's very nice of you to say." Composed as she was, Ross didn't miss that she was blushing, an adorably endearing reaction given how gorgeous she looked.

The movie forgotten, Sam rose up on her knees and peered over the sofa back. "Those are really good shoes. Can I borrow them sometime?"

"Absolutely not," Ross answered for her.

Martha Jane sent him a smile. "I hope this is formal enough."

She gestured to indicate the simple but stunning dress. Or maybe it was just a regular dress and the thing that made it so eye-popping was that it was wrapped around her. She would look terrific in a bag—or, better yet, a bed sheet.

"You're...perfect," Ross said, his gaze going down to her legs.

Long and shapely, until now they'd been half hidden by the modest knee-length hemlines she usually wore. Their sudden bareness seemed to hint at a host of possibilities, most of them rated R. What would it feel like to slide a hand upward along her silky thigh and investigate whether or not the getup included lacey black garters? He jerked himself from the hinterlands of fantasy. What was the matter with him? This woman was his housekeeper and Sam's de facto nanny. She'd kindly consented to help him out by being his dinner date for the evening. She deserved his utmost consideration, restraint, and respect, and instead he was behaving—misbehaving— like a hormone-crazed adolescent who'd just gotten hold of his first Victoria's Secret catalogue.

The soft smile she sent him did funny things to his insides. "Thanks. So do you, very dashing."

He tugged on his French cuffs though, like the rest of the tuxedo, they hit exactly where they were supposed to. Growing up, he'd never expected to own his own tux, let alone an Armani. Back then he would have assumed Armani was an Italian pasta dish.

A mental picture of his first rental, the powder blue polyester with a ridiculously ruffled shirt he'd worn to his junior prom, flashed into his awareness, and it occurred to him he should spend more time being grateful for just how far in life he'd come.

He glanced down at his watch. "The cocktail reception starts at six." Hating small talk, he usually skipped the drinks prelude to the evening and arrived for the dinner seating, but now he found himself looking forward to it all. Glancing back at Samantha, he said, "Do your old man a favor and don't burn down the building while we're gone." Ignoring Sam rolling her eyes, he turned and offered Martha Jane his arm. "Shall we?"

• • •

Held in the historic Hay-Adams Hotel in Lafayette Square, the Heritage Foundation dinner started like a Cinderella evening. Staring out the car window at the grand Italian Renaissance-styled landmark, the path from curb to colonnaded entrance draped in red carpet, Macie had to remind herself that she was on a mission and that nothing about this night was real. Not for her.

Handing his keys to the parking valet, Ross climbed out, came around to the passenger's side, and opened the car door.

"Nervous?" he asked, offering Macie his arm.

"A little," she admitted. Stepping out amidst the flash of cameras, she took a moment to smooth her skirt before tucking her arm in his.

Though she'd covered celebrity events in New York, she'd never actually walked a red carpet before. Being at center stage versus observing from the sidelines was definitely a different feeling.

"You don't need to be." Reaching over, Ross laid his free hand atop hers. "You're stunning." The smile he flashed brought out the cute crinkles at the corners of his eyes.

Heat hit her in the face for the second time that evening, and she could no longer ignore the obvious. She was blushing. Just when had she become a blusher? Was she playing her part so well that she was actually becoming Martha Jane Gray? Or was it that being with Ross Mannon brought out the hopeful girl she'd once been, the one she'd put so much energy and effort into burying?

She ducked her head, the sudden shyness in no way feigned. "Thank you. That's very kind."

If she had to deal with embarrassment, at least she wasn't alone. Reddening, Ross held his gaze on hers. "It's not kindness, it's the truth." He looked away. "The banquet's being held at The Top of the Hay on the ninth floor. I haven't been up there before but the views should be pretty nice."

As always, retreating into character was the best way she knew of grounding herself. Deliberately goggle-eyed, she asked, "Do you think we'll see Newt Gingrich?"

Ferrying her toward the arched doorway and inside the ornate lobby, Ross hesitated, looking a lot less enthused than she would have expected. "If he's in town, he's probably here."

"Ooh, do you think he'd let me take his picture for my momma? She just loves Newtie."

The look he sent her was positively pained. "I don't know. I can ask him…although to be honest, I'm not really a fan."

That surprised her. "Because you disapprove of his personal life or you dislike his politics?"

Ross didn't hesitate. "Both," he said, steering them toward the elevator.

Cramming on with the other formally attired guests, she bumped against a distinguished elder statesman.

"My apologies, young lady," he said in a gravelly Kansas accent, though it had probably been her fault.

Still, this was too good an opportunity to pass up. She waited for the elevator doors to close and then turned to Ross and announced in a deliberately high whisper, "Oh… my… goodness! I just brushed Bob Dole. Bob Dole! Yowza!"

The retired U.S. Senator and former presidential candidate was indeed the gentleman standing close by. Catching his eye, she shot him a very "Macie Graham" wink. She was probably—okay, definitely—overdoing the hayseed act, but she was having so much freakin' fun, why stop? She glanced over at Ross, expecting him to be mortified. Instead the corners of his mouth twitched. Damn, but he wasn't mortified at all. Far from it, he was holding back…laughter!

The cocktail reception was in full swing when they stepped inside. Ross snagged two glasses of champagne from a passing server and they moved about the room, mingling while a pianist played standards such as "Stormy Weather" and hits from various Andrew Lloyd Weber musicals. A sit-down dinner in the Thomas Jefferson Room followed. Beautiful mosaic tiles laced with vines and rich pale marble provided an understated yet elegant backdrop for the eight top tables covered in sumptuous cream and gold linens, each crowned with a floral centerpiece of red and white roses. A skylight and floor-to-ceiling windows opened out onto the terrace from which the White House, Lafayette Park, and St. John's Church could be seen.

The dinner service about to begin, Ross led Macie to their table at the room's front. Their five tablemates, already seated, were all other award recipients and spouses, he explained. Introductions were made, ranging from stiffly polite to warmly cordial. Macie shook hands with the president of an Ivy League university, an iconic film actor known for his cop and cowboy roles, and a retired Supreme Court justice. Macie hated to admit it but she was impressed—and shy at being so out of her element.

Subsiding into the chair Ross held out, she glanced to the sole unclaimed seat. "It seems we have a mystery guest," she whispered.

Was it her imagination or did he stiffen? "Sometimes contributors buy seats to get their names on the program and then arrive late or not at all," he said, dropping into the chair beside her. His voice sounded almost...hopeful.

Pre-printed menu cards were provided for each place setting. The meal would comprise five courses, each dish prepared by a different chef and paired with a unique wine. Macie could see she'd be skipping the first course, a white truffle-infused foie gras mousse. She might not be a vegetarian but eating the livers of force-fed geese was too much bad karma to risk bringing down.

A silent army of tuxedo-clad servers appeared bearing bottles of chilled white wine and silver trays with their first courses. Ross passed Macie the bread basket. "If you somehow haven't noticed, I'm a meat and potatoes man—and I like to think my meat has had a decent life, or at least a fair fight." He slanted a loveably lopsided smile and Macie felt her heart warming.

"Thanks," she said, taking a roll and picking off a pat of

the rose-sculpted butter.

After the foie gras, things looked up. Overall the food was far better than the rubber chicken Macie had expected. Then again, at eight thousand dollars a plate and sixty grand a table, it ought to be. They were just finishing their entrée of sake-marinated black cod when Macie spotted a tall, striking brunette striding toward them. Even from half a room's length away, Macie instantly recognized the floor-scraping black chiffon gown as Dior—and its wearer as internationally famous fashion photographer Francesca St. James.

Resisting the impulse to slink low in her seat, she took a deep drink of pinot grigio and focused on clinging to her calm. There was no point in being paranoid. She'd met the Brit just once—and briefly—the year before on a fashion shoot for the magazine. Shooting the spring fashion issue in Central Park in mid-winter had tested everyone's patience, especially that of the gooseflesh-covered models, but Francesca had been unfailingly upbeat and professional, somehow managing to evoke everyone's best work despite record-breaking cold and the caterer running out of coffee. At the time Macie had been rocking a retro red spiral perm and glitzed out grunge vintage wear. With her new look, surely Francesca wouldn't recognize her.

Ross pushed back his chair and politely rose. "Frannie, you're just in time for dessert."

Frannie? It took Macie a moment to put it all together but once she did...Ross's ex-wife was Francesca St. James? Holy shit, it couldn't be...could it? Macie glanced at Ross to gauge his reaction but beyond a barely noticeable deepening color in his cheeks, his expression was impassive.

Francesca struck a casual pose that accentuated every nuance of the body-grazing gown and the apparently cellulite-free figure beneath it. "Darling, do I look as though I eat dessert?"

"Good point," he said, leaning in to kiss her offered cheek.

Watching them, Macie felt her mood flag and not only because she feared discovery. Ross's ex was everything Macie wasn't, the real deal, not a chameleon, not a fake. Unlike Macie, Francesca didn't have to chase trends or hide behind costumes. She was her own woman and she set her own style. Alongside her, Macie felt not so much understated as dowdy, especially with her vintage red shoes, her statement accessory—the one material thing that made her feel like… *her*—hidden beneath the table.

Ross stepped back and pulled out the vacant chair. "Coffee, then?"

Fabric swished as Francesca gracefully slid into the offered seat. "An espresso would be divine."

"I'll see what I can do." He turned and beckoned for their server.

Francesca's cool, catlike gaze studied Macie from across the cloth-covered table. "You must be the house—Ross's date."

"Yes, I'm Martha Jane."

"Ross mentioned you recently relocated from New York. Pardon me for asking, but have we met before?"

Macie shook her head. "I suspect we travel in very different circles." A glamorous fashion photographer and a humble housekeeper would have little chance of meeting socially.

Francesca's red mouth pursed. "Darling, I'm a photographer. I may forget a name but never a face, especially one as striking as yours."

Heart thrumming, Macie shrugged. "They say everyone has a body double."

French manicured nails lightly drummed the tabletop.

Francesca's gaze held. "No matter, it will come to me in time."

Macie thought again of Francesca's *On Top* shoot. The Brit was a consummate professional, not a diva but certainly a perfectionist. From one model's slightly feathered lipstick to the dime-sized wad of frozen chewing gum marring their otherwise pristine park path, no detail had escaped her. It was only a matter of time before Francesca remembered her and the other shoe—make that red slipper—dropped.

The chicory aroma of freshly brewed coffee filled the space. Trays of desserts were passed about. The emcee stepped up to the podium.

"Tonight is a very special evening to honor those individuals and program initiatives that exemplify the American values and principles that the Heritage Foundation has espoused since our founding in 1973. For his tireless—and at times spirited—defense of the American family, we honor Dr. Ross Mannon as our Republican of the Year. Dr. Mannon, please join us onstage to accept our sincere thanks—and your award."

She snagged Ross's gaze and, going with her gut, she smiled. This time it wasn't Martha Jane who smiled. It was Macie, all Macie. Beneath the table, he suddenly reached for her hand and squeezed it. And then just as suddenly, he was breaking hands and pushing away from the table, standing and striding through the aisle between tables to the podium. Gaining it, he turned to face the seated audience, his grace and aplomb stealing her breath. He shook the presenter's hand and accepted the statuette.

Drawing the microphone toward his mouth, he began. "My fellow Americans, the greatest American virtue can be summed up in a single word: character. Our unflappable integrity, our honesty…"

Integrity, honesty…suddenly Macie knew that if she

stayed to hear the end of his acceptance speech, she'd never be able to go through with it. Operation Cinderella would be as good as finished and her career with it. She had to get away and think.

She shot up from her seat, bumping against the table and causing coffee to slosh onto the expensive linens. Dodging Francesca's surprised stare, she grabbed her evening clutch and made a beeline for the exit.

She could catch a cab back to Ross's condo. Later she could say she'd felt suddenly sick. It wasn't far from true. She made it through the hotel lobby and outside to the cab queue before her right foot gave way. What the fuck? Bending down, she saw the velvet-covered heel had split straight through—so much for any supposed fairy-tale magic or silver screen mojo.

Tears welled. Wishing she'd thought to wear waterproof mascara, she forced them back. When had she suddenly become so stupidly sentimental? It was only a shoe, after all, not a dream and certainly not a fairy tale.

A hand touched her shoulder. She whirled, losing her balance.

Ross caught her against him. "Hey, princess, is it Pumpkin Time so soon? Can't be, it's not even midnight."

Never so glad to be caught in her life, it was all Macie could do to say, "I'm afraid I've had a wardrobe malfunction."

He followed her gaze downward. "That's a shame. I know a really great shoe repair place. They can't help you tonight, but we can drop them off tomorrow first thing."

His casual mention of "we" warmed her, as did leaning into his big, strong body; the latter felt unbelievably nice. "Thanks."

"You're welcome." He hesitated and then wrapped an arm about her waist. The heat from his palm seemed to sear the black silk. His other hand held his statuette.

"Congratulations again on your award. I'm sorry I missed the rest of your speech."

He shrugged as if the accolade was a trifle. "I'm sorry I had to leave you in the lions' den. Was Frannie okay? Did she play nice?"

Macie hesitated. "She can be a little...intense."

He stopped, threw back his head and laughed. "That's a pretty big understatement."

"For what it's worth, I really admire her. She's smart, witty, and talented, not to mention gorgeous." It was all true, of course. She watched Ross's face, waiting for him to agree.

Instead he lifted one sandy brow and said, "I'm sensing there's a 'but' in there somewhere."

There was indeed. Still, Macie hesitated. "She's not exactly who I would have pictured you marrying." Wondering if she'd gone too far, she bit her bottom lip, a nervous habit that "Martha Jane" and "Macie Graham" unfortunately sometimes shared. "I shouldn't have said that."

Ross shook his head. "No apology necessary. Hindsight being twenty-twenty, I have trouble picturing it myself." He chuckled, the sound setting Macie once more at ease—or at least as eased as one could be in the midst of pretending to be someone else. "Listen," he said, keeping a bolstering hold on her elbow, "I know you've thrown a shoe and probably can't go far, but Washington really is a beautiful city, especially at night. What do you say to me busting the car out of valet and us going somewhere quieter where you can see it?"

•

Macie stood alone with Ross on the Kennedy Center's rooftop terrace, flutes of champagne in hand and the panorama of Washington, DC and Virginia spread out before them. To the southeast she picked out the dome and classical colonnade of the Jefferson Memorial and the obelisk of the Washington Monument. To the north was the distinctive cylindrical Watergate complex where Ross lived. Myriad lights twinkled from Georgetown's Washington Harbor, making the historic seaport seem like a fairy-tale village in miniature. More lights outlined the Memorial Bridge leading across the river to Virginia. Seen from this vantage point, the Potomac looked like a giant reflecting pool, the sort you saw in the older enclosed shopping malls from the seventies and eighties, the basin bottoms covered in pennies hurled by the hopeful.

Make a wish, Martha Jane.

Glancing up to the sky lit with stars and ambient light, Macie wished with whatever heart she still had that she could change—for the night at least—who she was and why she'd come.

"Cold?" Ross's question called her back to the moment.

The evening breeze held just enough of a hint of fall to bring gooseflesh to her bare arms. "A little," she admitted, "but it's too beautiful to go inside just yet."

She'd been to the famous performing arts center just once before as a student, when a kindly college professor had handed over her extra ticket to a production of "Shear Madness" held in the Theater Lab, but the terrace had been temporarily closed. Struggling to balance her coursework with part-time jobs, Macie hadn't been able to come back. Now, owing to Ross, she was standing on the marble-covered terrace sipping champagne and wearing black silk, albeit in bare feet.

"Here, take my jacket," he said, slipping it off. Overriding her protests, he draped it across her shoulders.

Hugging it around her, she took a moment to savor the slight scent of sandalwood and the warmth that the fabric had absorbed from his big, strong body. Feeling borderline breathless, she looked away to the statuette of Lady Liberty set atop one of the lounge tables. "Where will you put her?" The trophy was a pretty impressive hunk of glass and gilded wood. The only person who didn't seem all that impressed was Ross. He'd actually suggested wrapping the award in an old towel and placing it in the trunk of his car.

"Not sure." He shrugged, the motion stretching his white tuxedo shirt across broad shoulders and a washboard flat belly.

Standing with him alone on the rooftop terrace, it was entirely too easy to imagine reaching up and unbuttoning that shirt, then slowly peeling it off. The vivid fantasy struck an inner alarm. She glanced down at her champagne, the fizzy wine already hitting below the half empty mark, and schooled herself to slow down. An almost two-week hiatus from her clubbing lifestyle had lowered her alcohol tolerance and she was buzzed, if not exactly drunk.

He took a sip of his champagne and stared out over the rail, and Macie took the opportunity to feast her gaze on the spare, clean lines of his profile. Whatever he might or might not be, Ross Mannon dressed in formalwear and drenched in moonlight made for a pretty heart-stopping view.

"All the awards in the world don't amount to a hill of beans without someone to share them with." He looked back at her. "Thank you for being that someone for me tonight."

Embarrassed, she dropped her gaze to her glass. "Sam's proud of you. That must count for something."

He shook his head. "I've been in her black books ever since I confiscated that damned magazine."

Macie winced. Not for the first time she wondered why one article on teenage sex had struck such a nerve with him.

Still, picking up on the hurt in his voice, she insisted, "No, really, she is."

"I'll have to take your word on it." He still sounded skeptical but the frown creasing his forehead smoothed.

She smiled up at him. Standing barefoot, she was shorter than he by at least a head. "I guess you will, Professor."

He smiled back, one broad hand braced on the balcony rail. "How about you start calling me Ross? Make it a habit or something?"

She pretended to consider. "We'll have to compromise," she finally said. "Ross it is, but only for tonight. And I'm...MJ. At least that's what my sister calls me. When Pam was little, Martha Jane was too much of a mouthful."

"MJ, I like it," he said, sending her a heart-stirring smile.

"But at the stroke of midnight, I go back to being the housekeeper and you to being *Doctor Mannon*."

He cocked a brow. "You drive a hard bargain, Cinderella. Midnight's just a few minutes away."

Caught up in the moment, she smiled back. "We should make the most of them then." God, had she really said that?

Resisting the urge to down the final few sips of champagne for the false courage it might bring, she surrendered her glass. He set it aside and then slipped his hand inside the jacket sleeve.

Finding her hand within, he gave it a light squeeze. "Seriously, I want to thank you for tonight and...for helping me remember what it feels like to feel."

His raw honesty melted the last of Macie's reserve. "That is quite possibly the nicest thing anyone has ever said to me."

Gaze locked on hers, he lifted the hand he still held and turned it over. "A woman like you should only ever have sweet things said to her, especially when they're all true."

The press of his mouth to her palm was shockingly erotic and sinfully sweet, and when the balcony seemed to sway,

Macie knew that her champagne buzz was in no way to blame. "Dr. Mannon?"

"It's not midnight yet. You promised to call me Ross." Releasing her, he slid his scarred workman's knuckles beneath her chin and tipped her face up to his.

He bent to her, closing the space between them. His breath was a cinnamon-spiced breeze against her cheek, his gaze moving over her the closest she'd come in a while to being caressed. At the first soft meeting of their mouths, a hot shiver shot through her. She shuddered, the motion sending his jacket slipping. His hands found the tops of her bare shoulders, the heat of his palms searing. She reached between them and wrapped an arm about his neck; the other took possession of his hard-muscled shoulder, her kneading fingers bunching the fine shirt fabric.

His hands slipped lower to the dress's plunging back, his fingers following the triangle cutout to the zipper. One tiny tug on the tab was all that it would take to free her.

"MJ," he breathed into her parted mouth, and the way he said the shortened version of her name sounded almost like a prayer—sanctified and serene, a promise that would carry them beyond the remaining minutes to midnight.

In the distance, a church bell chimed, one, two, three…

It was pumpkin time, or certainly a call back to sanity. Macie broke off the kiss and stepped away, her arm slipping from his shoulder and pushing against the hard beating heart on the left side of his chest. "I'm sorry, I can't."

He released her and backed away. He shook his head as if to clear it, drew a shuddering breath, and then swallowed so deeply it looked as if his Adam's apple might leap free from his throat. "No, I'm the one who's sorry. I was wrong to take advantage. It's late and we both have early mornings. I should get you home."

Chapter Seven

He had her, she was his, her body and will trapped within his unbreakable embrace, the long, loose sleeves of his black cassock wrapping around her like bat wings, the cold metal crucifix cutting into her breast. His mouth covered hers, suckling to silence her breath and her screams, her fight and her freedom. She stilled to a statue, finally accepting the terrible truth. She might be an honor roll student, the acknowledged "popular girl" of her sophomore class, and a two-time finalist in her state's spelling bee, but she wasn't going to win this one. Now that it really counted, now that the stakes were as high as the New York skyscrapers she hoped one day to see, she wasn't going to win.

The fact was she'd already lost. She'd lost the moment she'd given in and let herself be goaded into following him back to the choir room after services. Now life as she'd known it—simple and sweet, slow-paced and secure—was over. The God she'd grown up learning to love and obey had deserted her to the darkness, relegated her to the mercy of the monster who every Sunday stood behind a pulpit and invoked His praises. From here on she had no beacon of light to look to, no happy future to plan. A bottomless pit of brimstone and blackness was home now. She was suffocating, drowning in it, and there was nothing and no one coming to her rescue. No Lord and Savior, no Prince Charming, no magic wand-wielding fairy godmother would find her in time. Even her body betrayed her. Like a fly caught in a spider's web, her arms and legs didn't work anymore. Struggling only made it worse, only made him worse. There was only one thing left for her to do.

She went limp and willed her mind to blankness.

Macie bolted upright in bed. For the first few sweaty, heart pounding seconds she didn't know where she was. Fortunately the room wasn't completely dark. It never was. She always slept with the bathroom light on. As much as she might like all-black clothing, all-black for the night was too terrifying to take.

She looked down to her legs tangled in the covers, and remembrance returned. Washington, DC; Ross Mannon's condo; Operation Cinderella. Far from reassuring, her reality seemed like yet another layer to the dreaded dream. *What am I doing?*

She glanced at the alarm. The backlit clock face showed 3:35 a.m. Her face was damp, her mouth dry. She could do with a drink of water but more than anything she needed a change of scene. Drawing deliberately deep breaths, she got up, pulled on her old Catholic U sweatshirt and a comfortably worn pair of jeans, and slipped out into the hallway. Passing Sam's closed door, she stepped out into the living room—and to the scent of strong coffee.

Ross stood at the kitchen counter, wearing a blue terrycloth bathrobe and a serious case of bed head. Cracking eggs into a bowl, he didn't seem to see her. Relying on the plush wall-to-wall to muffle her retreat, she whipped around—and slammed into the coffee table.

"F— Ouch!"

Ross's head shot up. Looking out into the living room, he said, "You okay?"

Bending down to rub her shin, she blew out a breath. "Great, thanks."

Seeing she was all right, he picked up the whisk. "Want some breakfast?"

Straightening, she answered, "Kind of early, isn't it?" As "Martha Jane" she would have taken care to be more polite. Unfortunately Macie Graham was in a ferociously bad mood—as well as pre-coffee.

He shrugged. "People who work on farms or oil rigs are sitting down to breakfast about now, so why not us?" He beckoned her over.

She hesitated, weighing her options: dream-haunted bedroom versus mortifying kitchen. Macie chose the kitchen. She walked up to the breakfast bar, pulled out a stool, and sat.

He handed her a steaming mug. "Thanks," she said, taking it.

It wasn't coffee but warm milk, the classic cure for insomnia. He'd even sprinkled nutmeg on top like her mom used to do. She wrapped both hands around the mug and took a sip. It was good.

He went back to beating the eggs. "I'm glad you're here. We need to talk."

"Please, can't we just...let it go?" Now especially, a post-mortem of her earlier humiliation was too much to take.

But Ross was adamant. "I need to apologize. I can't find strong enough words to tell you how deeply I regret my behavior. It was appalling, totally out of line. Honestly, I don't know what came over me. I don't go around kissing—"

"The help?" she put in. She wasn't sure which was worse: having accepted a pass from a Republican or hearing he wasn't that into her.

"Young women who work for me," he corrected. "You have my word it won't happen again."

She tried for a smile but it felt brittle and stale, as though it might flake off at any moment. Despite the embarrassment and tension that had followed, so far as she was concerned the kiss had been altogether awesome, the hands down best of her life. Hearing how much he regretted it ruined even that.

"Thanks, but if it helps, it was just a kiss. It's not like you ravished me." She had the satisfaction of seeing him pale. "And I'm as much to blame as you. I kissed you back. But you're right, it was a mistake. For Sam's sake, I think it's best if we set it aside and move on, don't you?

She slipped off the stool and stood. Maybe bolstered by the warm milk, her room wouldn't feel so forbidding.

But it seemed Ross had other plans. "Sit yourself right back down."

Macie prided herself on being immune to orders, so it was a big surprise to her when she obeyed.

Dropping the whisk, he braced both hands on the counter, eyeing her. "We've been circling each other like cats ever since you first set foot inside this apartment, and I at least need to settle things so I can get back to sleeping nights."

He was losing sleep over her? Considering the bruising her ego had taken during his "apology," knowing that thoughts of her kept him awake was pretty vindicating.

She laced her hands around the mug to hide their trembling. "I'm listening."

"The thing is, I like you, MJ. I like you a lot. What's more, I think you may like me, too. And if it's all right with you, I wouldn't mind seeing where that mutual liking might take us. But I don't want to do anything to scare you off or make you feel like you have to leave here, because Sam needs you. So if you don't feel the same about me, just say the word, and I'll back off."

Macie's gaze flew to his. The vulnerability she saw clawed at her heart. He liked her. He really liked her! And yet how much of what he was feeling was for the real her and how much was for Martha Jane? There was only one way to find out. Looking across the counter to him, so earnest and honorable and sexily rumpled, she dared to consider putting journalistic ambition on the back burner. Maybe with a man like Ross Mannon things could work out differently than they had in the past. Maybe things could work out—period. Maybe it was time she stepped away from the safety net of her cynicism and gave this whole happiness thing an actual shot.

She set down the mug. "I don't want you to back off."

He swallowed hard. "You don't?"

"No, I don't." Before he might say more, she stood, reached over the breakfast bar—and opened his robe.

. . .

Staring down, Ross was shocked—and turned on as hell. For a sweet, old-fashioned girl, MJ sure had some moves on her.

He caught her wrist before she got a handle on his hard-on. "Slow down. Where's the fire?" It took every iota of his willpower, but he managed to move her hand away.

She stared up at him, looking all kinds of confused. "I don't get you. One minute you want me, the next you don't."

The pained expression on her lovely flushed face very nearly undid him—nearly but not all the way. Determined to stay strong for both their sakes, he shook his head. "Of course I want you. I want you more than you probably even know. But I also don't want to rush things and screw up any chance we have of making this into something more than a fling."

He and Francesca had jumped into bed—actually, the backseat of his borrowed Ford truck—without taking the time to get to know each other first. With their teenage hormones hopping, casual sex had seemed like a fine idea, but he'd always wondered if things might have turned out differently if they'd waited. He'd never know the answer, but what he *did* know was he was coming to care too much about MJ to take anything about her casually.

She eased back onto the stool. "So what's next?'

He'd half expected her to run back to her room. Relieved when she didn't, he said, "What's next is breakfast. Ever had huevos rancheros?"

"Once, I think. On second thought, maybe not." She hesitated and then said, "Do you seriously expect me to sit here and bolt down a big breakfast after the monumental ass I've just made of myself?"

He grinned at her and reached for another egg to break. "Darlin', some people would say I make an ass of myself every time I go on air."

• • •

Macie didn't have a comeback for that, so she kept quiet and watched him neatly crack three more eggs in quick succession. "Have you never heard of cholesterol?" she asked, watching him pour a generous measure of half-and-half into the mix.

"I focus on the calcium." He picked up the whisk and resumed beating the mixture into froth. "Besides, the meals you've been serving haven't exactly been low-fat."

He had her there. "I thought that was the kind of food you liked, coming from Texas."

"I do, only I'm closer to thirty-five than thirty, and since moving here I don't get nearly the exercise I used to."

Macie's gaze dropped to his midriff, which she strongly suspected was a perfect six pack or close to it, and suddenly she felt as if she stood inside a steaming shower, her body moist and tingling.

He rinsed off the whisk and set it on the sink drainer. "We don't have any avocados, so I can't make it with guacamole, but I found a jar of chili peppers in the cupboard and we have sour cream and cheese. The grater's over there." He gestured to the cutting board where a hunk of Monterey Jack set out.

Amazingly, she was hungry. She sliced off a piece of cheese and popped it into her mouth before turning to grate the rest into a small bowl.

He grabbed a fistful of cutlery and carried it and their plates out to the table along with a bottle of Tabasco. In addition to the hot milk, he'd made a pot of coffee. Macie mused it must be a Texas thing, the way he could suck down gallons of the stuff at all hours. Ordinarily her morning tall skinny soy latte was all she needed to carry her through the day. Then again it was, technically, morning.

"Sure." She held out her empty mug, and he refilled it.

Sour cream, half-and-half, and real butter! She forked up a big bite and closed her eyes, taking the time to savor. "This is so…good it's got to be bad." Guard down, she'd almost said *fucking good* but stopped herself in time.

Ross chuckled. "Everything in moderation, right?" Moderation wasn't a subject on which Macie had ever excelled, but she nodded anyway and took another mouthful. "Besides," he added, watching her eat, "it's not like you have to count calories."

His gaze stroking over her was as powerful as a tactile touch. Fortified by food and caffeine, sex once more pushed to the forefront of her mind.

Feeling the telltale tremulousness return along with a

rather deliciously warm tingling, she put down her fork. "I'd rather burn them than count them. Are you sure you won't reconsider your stance on flings?"

The look he slanted her told her to give it up. "If you're trying to shock me, you're wasting your time. I was a daddy when you were still in training bras."

"I never wore training bras."

She stared at him. He stared back. And then the weirdest thing happened. The corners of her mouth started to twitch, the back of her throat to tickle. Something, some tight ball of tension, bubbled and then burst inside her. Macie threw back her head and laughed. Her eyes watered, her throat burned, and still she laughed. And the best part was Ross joined her.

"Okay...okay," she said once she'd mustered sufficient breath. Swiping at her watering eyes, she willed the fit to subside. "Maybe I did, but just for that one year in middle school."

He winked, and then rose to refill his mug. "Your secret's safe with me."

His mention of secrets had her remembering hers. Operation Cinderella was stymied, but she couldn't think about that now.

He'd rejected her for the second time in an hour. She had every right to feel pissed as hell, not to mention hurt. But along with a vague disappointment, what she felt was relaxed—and suddenly sleepy.

She covered a yawn behind her hand. "Mind if I leave the dishes for the morning, the *real* morning, and go back to bed?"

"Go ahead. It's my mess. I'll clean it."

She pushed her chair back from the table and got up. "Good night then."

She was almost to the living room when he called her

back. "MJ?"

Even half asleep, her heart skipped when he called her nickname. She turned around. "Yes."

Crossing the carpet toward her, he said, "About my apology earlier—don't go getting the wrong impression."

Her heart seemed to stall. "What wrong impression might that be?"

He stopped in front of her. "That I didn't like kissing you. Fact of the matter is I liked it a lot." He took a final step toward her, one big warm hand closing gently over her shoulder. "And just because you're going back to your bed and I'm going back to mine doesn't mean I wouldn't like to try it again—now."

She tilted her face up to his. Reaching out, he traced the outline of her bottom lip with the callus-thickened pad of his thumb. Hot chills skipped along her spine. Her heart pounded and her breath caught. She felt famished, only not for food but for Ross.

Their mouths met as if drawn by magnets. His kiss was tangy with Tabasco and passionate with promise. His tongue slipped inside to touch hers, a gentle tease. But suddenly gentle wasn't enough anymore. Ravenous, she wanted more.

She wanted it all.

As if reading her mind, he moved his hand to her nape, gently but firmly holding her in place while he plundered. Her nipples tightened, making her keenly aware that she hadn't bothered with a bra. As if reading her mind, he slid his other hand beneath the waistband of her sweatshirt, skimming the well of her belly and playing along her ribs before sliding slowly upward. The brush of his thumb over her breast shot an arrow of sensation straight to her toes.

Touching her beneath her clothes, he drew back to nip at her neck. "No, ma'am, definitely don't need any training bra now."

He grazed her nipple, the slight roughness of his fingers making her moan. She threw back her head and pushed against his palm. "That feels...entirely...too...good to even think of stopping."

His soft laugh resonated with male pride but the erection brushing against her lower belly confirmed he was as turned on as she. "In that case, we should probably say good night."

"Good night?" Macie clutched at his hand, hoping to stay him. Was Ross Mannon a clit tease or was he simply trying to kill her?

He pulled her sweatshirt back down and stepped back with an expression of regret. "Sweet dreams, baby."

Sweet dreams—suddenly that seemed like a distinct possibility.

"This is so unfair," she said, but the smile in her voice wasn't lost on either of them. Senses singing, she turned to go, intimately aware of his gaze following her out.

Stepping inside her room, she felt herself smiling. Warm milk, spicy eggs, and now a first rate make out session—if that wasn't the "complete package" Macie couldn't say what was.

•

"You're unusually cheerful," Stef remarked during her drop-off later that day.

Macie halted her humming. "Am I?"

"Uh huh."

"The food looks amazing," Macie said, deliberately turning the topic, although it was nothing less than the truth. The dinner menu du jour, boneless braised beef ribs, sautéed white asparagus, and rice pilaf, looked and smelled mouth-watering.

"About ten minutes before you serve, heat up the meat in the oven, not the microwave. That way it's less likely to dry out," Stefanie advised.

Macie nodded. "Okay, I will. Thanks."

Her insulated case emptied, Stef turned to go. "Bon appétit."

Screwing up her nerve, Macie called her back. "Are you in a big hurry?"

Stefanie stopped and turned back. "I have to deliver some party platters later, but I have some time. What's up?"

Macie reached for her nerve. "I was wondering if you might walk me through making huevos rancheros."

Stef's dark eyes widened. "You want me to show you how to *cook* something?" She came up, stuck out a hand, and made as if to check Macie's forehead for fever.

Batting her away, Macie backed up. "What if I do? Lately I've developed...a craving." That was oh so true.

Shrugging off her windbreaker and dropping it atop one of the stools, Stef ticked off the list of ingredients. "Eggs, salsa, sour cream, grated cheese, olive oil, and scallions, very finely chopped. Oh, and you'll need corn tortillas, of course."

Macie nodded. "Ross keeps tortillas in the fridge like other people keep sandwich bread. Must be a Texas thing," she added with a smile.

"Great, we'll need one tortilla per serving. Oh, and I like to include guacamole—that's mashed avocado, by the way." Stef winked.

"Very funny, yes, I know." Macie had stopped off at the grocery store after dropping Sam at school, gathering the ingredients she'd committed to memory. She opened the fridge and began setting them out.

She lined up the items on the counter and turned back to see her friend had taken the large frying pan down from its wall hook. Pouring olive oil in the pan, she turned the stove burner to low.

"It's a cinch so long as you follow the recipe," Stef assured her, rotating the pan so the bottom was evenly coated.

Macie came up beside her. "It's me you're talking to, remember? A card carrying member of the culinary-impaired."

"You'll do great. Most of the work is in the prep. I usually make my salsa from scratch but with a little doctoring, readymade salsa can work, too."

Macie thought back to that morning. While certain... *details* were tattooed onto her brain, she was fuzzy on the cooking part. "I'm pretty sure Ross used salsa from a jar."

Stef's gaze flew up from the sizzling pan. "Mannon made you breakfast?"

Recalling Ross's tangy kiss and knowing touch, Macie felt her face flame. Hoping Stef would attribute any flushing to the rising steam, she answered, "It was a case of mutual insomnia leading to the munchies."

"Interesting," Stef said, handing Macie the spatula. Macie stared at it. "You asked me to walk you through, right? What are you waiting for, rookie? Let's get started."

Nervous, nonetheless Macie did her best to follow Stef's directions to the letter, occasionally pausing to ask a clarifying question such as the difference between chipotle and chili powder and how long to cook the tortillas on each side.

Cooking the eggs proved to be the easy part. Apparently there were two versions of the dish, one with scrambled eggs, as Mannon had made, and the other with fried. Feeling brave, Macie decided to try fried. In the same skillet she'd used to heat the tortilla, she followed Stef's directions and added a dollop of butter. She waited a moment for it to melt, and then cracked in two eggs.

"Cook them for three to four minutes if you want the yolks runny, longer if you like them firmer," Stef advised.

"Definitely firmer," Macie said, picking out a piece of shell.

At the end of twenty minutes give or take, Macie had a nearly perfect plate of huevos rancheros.

Beaming, Stef handed her a fork. "You did it, Mace!"

"I did it, didn't I?" Absurdly excited, Macie picked up a fork and dug in. Popping the morsel into her mouth, she chewed, savored, and finally swallowed. Setting down the fork, she felt a big grin breaking forth. "I made this and it doesn't suck. It's actually pretty good."

"Of course it is." Stef patted her on the shoulder. "The act of cooking can be a very powerful thing. It's no coincidence that 'holy days' became our modern holidays and that the celebrations always involved sharing beautifully prepared food." She hesitated, and then asked, "This sudden...*craving* for Tex Mex wouldn't have anything to do with a certain hot Texas transplant, would it?"

Caught out, Macie admitted, "He's not anything like what I came here expecting. He's warm and funny and kind and caring. He even helps out around the house."

Equally amazing was her discovery that there were some aspects of domestic life she actually enjoyed, such as family movie night with Ross and Sam passing around a big bowl of popcorn and arguing over how much salt to add. Ross's daughter might have some issues, but now that she'd started letting down her guard on occasion, she was a pretty cool kid. Helping her with her homework and chauffeuring her around the city could even be fun.

"Sounds like a keeper. And he's single, right?

Macie nodded. "Divorced, but it happened years ago. He must have married pretty young." She declined to point out that Ross's ex was a famous fashion photographer whom she'd first met at the magazine. Stef didn't keep up with the fashion world, so the name Francesca St. James likely would mean nothing to her.

"So what's the problem?"

"Well, for starters, he's a Republican."

Her friend shrugged. "You say that like some people say 'axe murderer.'"

"There's a difference?"

"Come on, Macie, lighten up. It is a two-party system." She popped a sliver of avocado into her mouth.

"Not if Ross and his followers have their way."

Stef lifted a dark slash of brow. "He has followers?"

"I'd say cronies but 'followers' has a nicer sound."

Obviously struggling to keep a straight face, Stef managed a nod. "Definitely makes him sound more messiah-like."

Macie rounded the counter and slumped down on a stool. "Seriously, Stef, what am I going to do? He thinks I'm someone I'm not, a sweet, old-fashioned girl who believes in the things he does. You and I both know that woman doesn't exist."

"Are you so sure about that?" Following, Stef sat down beside her. "If you mean the woman who just learned to make huevos rancheros even though she claims she hates to cook and who talks my ear off about some teenage kid who's not hers but who she worries about all the time anyway, then I'd say she exists all right."

Macie speared her with a look. "You know why I came here."

"Muckraking mission, Operation Cinderella, yep, I copy you. So bag the Black Ops and move on. Mannon sounds like he just may be a pretty great guy. There aren't all that many of them out there." She sighed.

"I'll lose my job at the magazine."

"There are other jobs at other magazines," Stef countered.

Macie shook her head. "Starr gave me my first byline. I'd still be covering the weather if it weren't for her. I owe her."

Stef scowled. "You've worked your ass off for her and that magazine for five years. Nobody *gave* you anything. You earned it all, paid your dues, and then some. The only person you owe now is yourself. You don't have to do this. You have choices, Mace. Make the most of them."

Appetite lost, Macie pushed the plate away. "It's a moot point anyway. Ross really is the Prince of Clean." The surety of her imminent failure to find anything approaching dirt, or even dust on Ross left her feeling simultaneously anxious and relieved.

"Then tell your boss the truth, that you've come up empty. Let the potato chips fall where they may and get on with your life—with or without *On Top* in it."

Stefanie was right, Macie decided. She might not have dirt but she did have a choice.

·

Standing outside the threshold to Sam's bedroom a week later, Macie hesitated, and then lightly knocked on the edge of the open door. "How's it going? About ready for a lunch break?"

"Almost." Gaze glued to her computer monitor, Sam beckoned her inside. "Check this out. It's my Social Studies project."

Entering, Macie said, "Not going so hot, huh?"

What was going well, very well, was Sam. Lately she'd begun keeping her bedroom door open during the day, a powerful symbol of all the ways she was opening up.

Dragging her gaze away from the screen, Sam admitted, "I could use some help."

Relieved it wasn't algebra again, Macie picked a path around the poster sized pieces of foam board, photos, scissors, and pushpins strewn across the carpet to Sam's desk. "What's the topic?"

"The American family. We're supposed to make a poster of our family tree. Mrs. Grant said to try and go back at least three generations for both our parents."

"Have you checked out the genealogy websites? You can search the immigration records for Ellis Island online, too."

"Thanks but actually I've got most of the old stuff already. It's Dad and Mom who don't make any sense."

Macie hesitated. "What do you mean?"

Sam poked a finger at the screen. "I was born on April 12, 1997. It says here that Mom and Dad didn't get married until September 1999."

Macie leaned in to look. Sam had landed on one of those amateur detective sites that catered to the paranoid and the nosy. For an annual membership of just $19.99, you could search and access the records of just about anyone for whom you had the most basic information.

Straightening, she stepped back. "These sites aren't always that reliable. Sometimes people have similar sounding names—"

"No, MJ, there's no mistake." Sam clicked on another window. "See? Here's the PDF of their marriage certificate, the one on file at the court house. That's my mom's signature. Believe me, she's written enough school notes for me to recognize it."

"Do you need the exact dates for your project?"

"Well, no, but—"

"Want my advice?"

Sam shrugged. "Sure."

"This project isn't for history, it's for social studies, so don't worry about exact dates right now. Finish your chart, turn it in to your teacher, and talk about this with your dad— in private. For now, let's go have lunch, okay?"

Looking up, Sam sent her a lopsided smile so like her dad's that Macie felt her heart fisting. "Let me guess, huevos rancheros?"

Now that Macie had learned how to make the dish, she couldn't seem to stop. She'd even started doing some grocery shopping on her own.

"Grilled cheese sandwiches, but I made them with gorgonzola."

Grinning, Sam got up from her seat. "Sounds fancy."

Macie put an arm around the girl's shoulders, pleased when Sam leaned in rather than pulled away. "Tell me about it. I'm a regular Rachel Ray."

That night Macie couldn't wait for dinner to end so she could see Ross alone, and not only to indulge in the private kisses they'd begun sharing in the evenings in his study. Closing the dishwasher, she sought him out.

Poking her head inside the open study doorway, she asked, "Have a moment?"

He looked up from his article draft, his pleased-to-see-her expression tugging at her heart. "As many as you want." He rose, rounded the desk, and reached for her.

She backed up a step. "It's about Sam." Reaching behind, she drew the door closed.

A worried look eclipsed his smile. "She seemed okay at dinner."

"She is okay. She's better than okay—she's great. She's also really smart." *Too smart for anyone's good, especially yours.*

"Sounds like one of us had better sit down."

They subsided into side-by-side chairs. Macie filled him in on Sam's Social Studies project and online discovery. Up until now, she'd expected him to deny it, to provide all sorts of proof pointing out the obvious, egregious mistake that had been made. Instead he sat almost perfectly still.

She reached over and touched his arm. "Ross?"

Staring ahead, he scarcely seemed to register her. "Frannie and I met the spring semester of my senior year when she came over as a foreign exchange student. Even as a skinny-assed eighteen-year-old, she had a way about her—bold as brass, sophisticated, worldly beyond her years. You would have thought she'd been with hundreds of guys, all of them James Bond."

Though she wanted to be supportive, Macie hadn't entirely gotten over her admittedly irrational jealousy of Francesca. The fashion photographer had always loomed as a larger than life figure, but lately she'd also become the competition. A first love was tough to beat. Listening to Ross rhapsodize was challenging, to say the least.

"We spent every day of that summer together, and those days flew by," he continued. "Before we knew it, it was the night before she was supposed to go back to England. I picked up a bottle of Boone's Farm and drove us out to the creek in my big brother's pickup. The thought of going to college still a virgin made me sick with shame. I'd figured her for a pro at sex, but in the end she'd confessed she'd never rolled on a condom either. The main event was about as relaxing as brain surgery though it was definitely shorter, five minutes tops. We didn't realize the condom had broken until after it was too late. Still, we convinced ourselves we'd be all right. I mean who gets pregnant their very first time? The next morning I drove her to the airport and put her on a plane to London."

He ran a hand through his mussed hair, causing the cowlick at the back to stand up, making him look like she imagined he must have at eighteen—earnest, confused, vulnerable.

"I didn't know Sam existed until I got Frannie's letter saying she'd had to drop out of Oxford, and by the way, we had a kid."

Suddenly his wacked-out reaction over her teen sex article made a sad sort of sense. She reached for his hand. "That must have come as quite a shock."

He snorted. "So much for my no strings attached summer fling. If it weren't for the photo she'd tucked inside, I think I might have torn up the letter and worked to convince myself she was playing me. But then I picked up that photo and there was Sam with Frannie's wavy dark hair and my wide mouth and mismatched ears and I just…" The rest of the words dropped off.

"Fell in love?" Macie finished for him, feeling herself tearing up.

"Yeah, which is how I found the guts to go to my parents and confess. They were madder than hell at me for being so irresponsible, but after the raucous died down, they loaned me the money I needed to bring Francesca and the baby back. We got married at a justice of the peace in a county where nobody knew me. Seeing as I'd been away at college, it was easy enough to put out the story that we'd eloped before Frannie left for England. Folks had their suspicions, of course, but my family's been in Paris for five generations and hell, it wasn't like we didn't end up doing the right thing."

"Meaning getting married?" There they were again, his old school values, as much a part of him as his hair or eye color.

"It sure as hell beat the alternative—having my baby girl grow up on the other side of the Atlantic and maybe getting to see her once a year if I was lucky. This way my mother could take care of Sam during the day so Frannie could go back to school. I'm not saying it was easy, but was it the right thing to do? Hell, yes."

The reporter in her couldn't resist adding, "And yet you ended up getting divorced." She slipped free of his hand.

He exhaled a long breath. "We got married to make a home for Sam…only home had started to feel more and more like a battleground with our daughter caught in the crossfire. Frannie felt like a fish out of water, not only culturally but professionally. She had her heart set on fashion photography, and there's not much in the way of haute couture in Paris, Texas. We separated when Sam was four, hoping we hadn't had the chance to screw her up too badly. I know this probably sounds weird, but after we divorced, I stared to remember all the things I'd liked about Francesca. She's smart and kind and funny in that dry, British way. You couldn't ask for a cooler head in a crisis or a better friend when the chips are down."

"She sounds pretty great. Sure you're not still in love with her?" Macie hoped she didn't sound as jealous as she felt.

He answered with a vigorous shake of his head. "Not by a long shot. She has faults, plenty of them. For starters, she can't stay in one place more than a month without getting antsy, which is one of the reasons being a photographer suits her. She gets to travel to locations all over the world, or at least to some of the prime parts of it."

"Great for her, not so good for Sam, I take it, hence the decision to have Sam stay with you semi-permanently?"

He shrugged. "Frannie's the first to admit she's not exactly a natural mother, but she'd give her life for that kid."

Just who was Ross Mannon? Despite his Texas good ol' boy demeanor, he didn't fit any stereotype Macie could come up with. Instead of trashing his ex-wife like many men would, he went out of his way to emphasize her positive points. Macie hadn't wanted to like Ross Mannon, hadn't even considered it a possibility. But unfortunately it was too late. She did like Ross. She liked him a lot. In fact, her liking was well on its way to becoming...a whole lot more.

"Most of the divorced men I've met aren't nearly so generous when describing their exes."

Zachary was one of them. He'd been married once and Macie didn't even know his ex-wife's first name. Whenever he'd spoken of her, he'd usually stuck to pronouns. And of course there was always "That Bitch."

Ross stretched, shifting his shoulders, the movement emphasizing their beautiful breadth. "Frannie's a neat lady. She's just not meant to be my lady."

Macie stood to leave. "You know Sam's going to come to you for answers sooner or later, and I'm betting on sooner. I suggested she hold off until after she turns in her project, but that's only a week or so away."

Ross rose as well. "Yeah, I do know it. What I don't rightly know is how I'm going to explain it all to her without risking whatever respect she still has for me."

His lost look tugged at her heart. "Tell her what you just told me, no sugar coating, just the straight facts. Okay, maybe skip the part about the Boone's Farm," she added with a chuckle.

He sent her a weary smile and shook his head. "There you go again, making me feel better when I would have reckoned that was damn near impossible."

They said their good nights at the closed study door with soft kisses and glancing caresses that, as always, left Macie wanting. "Good night," she said, lifting her lips from Ross's with the usual regret.

He dropped a kiss atop her nose and stepped back with an

audible sigh. "Sleep well, princess. I'll see you in the morning."

Princess! If only he knew that her true colors weren't princess pastels but wicked witch black.

Back in her room, Macie sat up in bed, mulling over her next move. A child born out of wedlock might not be the major dirt she'd started out envisioning, but with the right spin, the story *could* stir a scandal, especially given Ross's strong stance against teen sex. With Sam's birth certificate and Ross and Francesca's marriage license accessible as public documents, there'd be no basis for a libel suit against the magazine or her personally. The situation was win-win, for her at least. So why wasn't she reaching for her laptop to pound out the story?

Several hours later and still awake, she finally faced her own inconvenient truth: Macie Graham had lost her edge. She'd broken the cardinal rule of investigative reporting and gotten involved with her subject. Fuck involved—she'd fallen for Ross. Her perspective on his radio show hadn't shifted one iota, but her perspective on the man had turned 180 degrees. Good and decent, honest and true, Ross Mannon was someone she'd be proud to call a friend—and someone she'd likely never be lucky enough to call more.

Clicking off the lamp, she reminded herself she should be on top of the world, dancing on a little pink cloud reserved all for her.

After weeks of fruitless searching, she'd finally found her story.

Chapter Eight

The following week seemed to crawl by and yet Macie's personal clock was ticking away like a bomb set to detonate. Entering her fourth week of Operation Cinderella, the tell-all story she owed the magazine was fast coming due. And any day now Francesca's fog could lift, and she would remember who Macie was and where they'd met. If she had anything resembling a brain, or guts, she'd pack up and leave before she dug in any deeper. But like a smoker trying to quit, she kept putting off the inevitable by "one more day."

She'd just set foot inside the apartment after dropping Sam at school when her cell phone went off. The ringtone, "Amazing Grace," was one she hadn't heard in quite a while.

It was the one she'd assigned to her mother.

There was only one reason her mother would pick up the phone and call her out of the blue. Something was wrong. Really wrong.

Heart slamming the wall of her chest, she pulled the phone from the bottom of her bag and answered. "Momma?"

"Martha Jane, thank the Lord." Her mother sounded on the verge of tears. Something was very wrong, indeed.

"Is it…Daddy?"

"It's your sister."

"Pammy!" Macie braced a hand against the wall, feeling as if the floor was suddenly melting beneath her feet.

Unlike her folks, she and her kid sister kept in close touch, or at least they had until a few months ago when Pam's calls, texts, and e-mails had dropped off. Other than exchanging a few text messages, they hadn't spoken in a month.

"She's in the hospital."

Her mother went on to explain that Pam had snuck out to a rave and someone had slipped Ecstasy into her soda. The drug reacted with the asthma medicine she'd taken, and she'd been rushed by ambulance to the medical center.

"She's asking for you, Martha Jane. I know how…*busy* you keep yourself in that city but is there any way you can come?"

"Of course I'll come. I'll call you back as soon as I figure out the details. For now, tell Pam I love her—and that I'm on my way."

Clicking off the call, she raced to her room for her laptop, turned it on, and started searching for flights. Fortunately Reagan National, the nearest airport, was less than a fifteen-minute drive.

While she searched, her reporter's mind sought to suss out the where, when, and how of the current nightmare situation—especially the *how*. When she'd last visited her folks, Pam had been a freckle-faced thirteen-year-old with a passion for basketball and a blissful obliviousness to boys. The thought of her baby sister at a rave, being pawed by boys and fed *drugs* had her breaking into a cold sweat.

"You okay?"

She looked up from her perch on the side of the bed to find Ross standing outside her doorway. She'd been so absorbed she hadn't heard him come in, let alone noticed his approach.

Her default response was that of course she was fine, but instead she shook her head and answered with utmost honesty. "Not really, no."

"Can I come in?"

Without warning, the lump in her throat exploded. "Please," she croaked, and then dropped her face into her palms, tears spilling.

Footsteps bounded toward her. Hands—big, strong, capable, and wonderfully warm—molded to her shuddering shoulders, stroked slow circles over her bowed back.

"Hey, easy there, honey. Whatever's wrong, I'm here. We'll figure it out together." He dropped down beside her. As many times as she'd imagined him in her room, in her bed, she'd never imagined it like this. "Talk," he said, wrapping a bolstering arm about her.

Curled against his chest, she recapped her mother's call.

"Of course you've got to go," he said as soon as she'd finished. "I'll drive you to the airport."

She scoured a hand across her eyes, which burned with tears and melted mascara. "Thanks, but I can call a cab."

"I'm driving you," he said in a tone that didn't allow for argument, and for once Macie wasn't really interested in arguing. The truth was she was starting to like that Ross was there to look out for her. She was liking it a lot.

With brisk efficiency, he began aligning the logistics. "You'll need a car once you land and there's no point in standing in a long line at the rental counter." He withdrew his wallet and pulled out his American Express Platinum Card.

"Ross, you are not paying for my flight or my rental car."

"Too late." He shouldered in closer, commandeered her laptop, and started punching at the keyboard. "I'm guessing we'd better book that flight one-way, not round-trip?" Saying the latter, his voice seemed to drop.

She nodded and pulled another tissue from the box. "Until I see Pam, see what we're dealing with, I won't know anything for sure."

He stopped what he was doing and put an arm around her shoulders. "She's asking for you, and that's a good sign. It shows she's conscious and alert."

Macie leaned in and rested her head on his shoulder, drawing from his strength, absorbing his calm. "I can't lose my little sister, Ross. I can't." Knowing that she stood to lose both Ross and Sam somewhere between the next few weeks and at any moment made that triply true.

He pressed a kiss atop her head. "I know, baby. I know."

But he didn't know, at least not yet. If he ever found out about Operation Cinderella, he wouldn't be able to bear breathing her air, let alone holding her like this. She tucked her head beneath his chin and hugged him hard. For all she knew, this might be the last time they were together like this—or together at all.

. . .

A few hours later, Ross let Macie out at the airline drop off. Popping his car's trunk and lifting the suitcase she'd hastily packed, he felt like the bottom had just dropped out of his life.

Determined not to show it, he plastered on a smile as if saying indefinite good-byes to important-to-him people was something he did every day. "Text me when you land, okay? And you need anything, anything at all, including someone to talk to, you call me, okay? I don't care what time of day or night it is—you call, you hear?"

She pulled up on her suitcase's retractable handle. "Okay,

I will. Thanks for…everything."

All around them, friends, families, and lovers embraced. Wishing they were the latter, wondering what they were or might yet become, Ross reached out to hug her.

Pressing a kiss to her temple, he said, "You take care of yourself and if you need anything, anything at all—"

"I'll call you, I promise."

Ross paused. Proceeding with caution was one thing, but suddenly it struck him that these past weeks he'd been more than cautious. He'd been running plain scared. *No guts, no glory, Mannon.* He leaned in to kiss her.

Honking startled them apart. Looking over her shoulder to the ferret-faced sedan driver laying on the horn, Ross had never wanted to murder someone half so much.

"I'd better get going." She flashed a quick smile and then turned away, rolling her suitcase toward the terminal entrance.

Resisting the urge to get in the sedan driver's face, instead Ross got back in the car. The front passenger's seat seemed sadly empty without her. Pulling out into the outgoing traffic lane, he asked himself—when had he come to need MJ so much?

But it wasn't until he stepped inside his condo that it hit him how empty the place felt without her. And it wasn't just the home-cooked meals, or the neatly picked-up rooms, or the security of knowing Sam was well looked after that he'd miss, great though all those things were. It was MJ herself. The way her smile lit up a room, the sound of her off-key humming, the way her sunshine clean scent lingered after she'd left. But what he'd miss most was the way she looked at him with those beautiful eyes of hers when he first walked in at night. That look made him feel ten feet tall and as strong as Atlas.

Get a grip, Mannon. She's not your wife. She's not even your girlfriend, not really.

But he was only kidding himself. In less than a month, Martha Jane Gray had become a whole heap more to him than that.

Along with Sam, she'd become pretty much his whole damned world.

. . .

Opening the front door, Macie's mother blinked tired eyes. "Martha Jane, you made it!"

Standing on her folks' front porch, Macie was struck by how old her mother seemed. The shrunken woman stepping out onto the stoop didn't much resemble the fire-and-brimstone-breathing dragon of her childhood or even of her last visit. Then Macie had shown up wearing a corset, black leather pants, and Goth boots, an overboard attempt to shock her parents. It had worked and yet, looking back, it seemed like a lot of wasted energy and effort.

The house, a single-story rambler with a croquet set and clothesline pitched on the front lawn looked pretty much the same as always, but the place no longer struck her as a prison. For the first time in more than a decade, happy memories returned to balance the bad. A truly horrible thing had happened to her here in her hometown, but a lot of pretty nice things had happened here, too—riding her bike for the first time without the training wheels; spending long, lazy summers planted on the front porch, playing flashlight tag and catching fireflies; picking out Pam from the sea of red-faced, squishy-headed newborns in this very hospital's neonatal nursery and proclaiming her to be "the prettiest baby ever."

On landing, Macie had gotten her mother's voice message that Pam had been discharged from the hospital. Grateful for the good news, if somewhat embarrassed at how quick she'd been to assume the worst, Macie had picked up the rental car and driven there directly from the airport. She bent to give her mother a quick kiss on the cheek.

Stepping back, she said, "I told you I was on my way."

Her mother nodded. "I know you did. I just can't believe it's...you." She held Macie at arm's length, surveying her with starved eyes. "You look so nice. You look so like...*you*."

Beyond pulling her hair into a ponytail and throwing on the first clothes she could find—a long-sleeved T-shirt and jeans—and shoving her feet into flat strappy sandals, Macie hadn't given her appearance much thought. No costume, no subterfuge, no manipulating her face and body to make any sort of statement.

Her mother ushered her inside the small living room. Taking stock of the pea green painted walls, sagging sofa, and faux oak entertainment console, Macie confirmed that not so much as a picture had been moved since her last visit. The observation struck her as strangely comforting. Then again, not everything about home had been bad. Memories of sacking out on that lumpy couch and watching Saturday morning cartoons on the TV's beveled glass screen came back to her, wrapped up with the aroma of pancakes frying on the griddle. As a kid, Sunday had been the Lord's Day, but Saturday had been focused on family—and fun.

Turning back to her mother, she asked, "Where's Dad?"

"He went to the pharmacy to pick up Pam's prescription. He'll be back in a bit."

"Is Pam in her room?"

Her mother nodded. "She's resting, but when I last looked in, she was awake. By the time the hospital doctor discharged her, you must have already boarded. You came all this way for nothing."

Tearing up, Macie shook her head. "Not for nothing,"

Her mother scoured a roughened hand across her own damp eyes. "I think knowing you were on your way helped with your sister's healing. It certainly lifted my heart." Her face crumpled. "Oh, Martha Jane, I know your father and I didn't do right by you all those years back, I know that now, but believe me, we love you to the bare bone. And we don't want to lose you again. Coming so close to losing Pam has made me see how bull-headed and blind I've been."

Tears trickled down Macie's cheeks. She didn't bother wiping them. Reminded of how Ross had hugged his daughter after she'd confessed to tampering with his computer, she hesitated and then opened her arms.

"Don't cry anymore, Momma." She enfolded her mother in a hug. Intending only to give comfort, she was taken aback by how good having her mother's arms around her felt after all these years. Drawing back, she said, "We'll talk more later. Right now, I'd really like to see Pam."

Her mother nodded. "You go on. I'll fetch you when Daddy's back."

Wiping her eyes, Macie headed to the back of the house where her sister's bedroom was. The door stood partway open. Before entering, she bolstered herself with a deep breath.

Pausing on the threshold, she called out, "Pammy?"

Pam lay propped up on pillows, her gaze glued to the small TV set atop the dresser, along with several stuffed animal toys. Her wan face was thinner than Macie remembered; the once silky blond hair twisted into snarled dreadlocks and tipped in fuchsia.

Pam shifted her gaze to the door. Her eyes lit. "MJ, you came!"

Macie walked up to the bed. "Of course I came."

"Momma said you would but I didn't believe her. You know her and her prayers." She rolled her eyes.

Just a few weeks ago, Macie likely would have joined her. Instead she said, "Maybe they worked." Pam scooted over to make room on the mattress, and Macie sat down on the edge.

Reaching out, she touched Pam's forehead, which felt fever free. "How are you feeling?"

Her sister shrugged. "Not so bad. My throat's pretty sore from the tubes and stuff and my stomach still hurts, but I'll live."

"Yes, you will. You were lucky. The next time you might not be."

Pam's smile dimmed. "Who says there's gonna be a next time?"

"I don't know, you tell me. Is there?"

Pam shook her head. "Nope."

"Why'd you do it, Pammy? You weren't a dumb kid when I left. You're not dumb now. But what you did, sneaking out like that, was dumb and dumber."

Pam bit her cracked bottom lip. "Yeah, I know. It's just so...boring here."

If Macie had lived closer, if she'd bothered to call more or visit once in a while, she might have steered Pam clear of some of the more serious adolescent pitfalls, warned her off making even one of the many mistakes Macie had. Instead she'd been too hell-bent on pursuing her Big City dreams to take the time, which made her a walking example of the kind of insular, postmodern selfishness Ross railed about on his show. Not for the first time she considered he might have a point.

"Maybe you could come and visit me in New York sometime."

Pam's eyes popped. "Could I? Do you think Momma and Daddy would let me?"

Not so very long ago, Macie would have replied no, never

in a million years, but having spoken with her mother, she was no longer so certain. Her mother had said she was sorry. If that could happen, almost anything was possible.

"They might. No promises, but I can talk to them about it—provided you absolutely one hundred percent promise me you'll never pull a stupid stunt like this again."

Pam's face lit. She stuck out her hand, the nails bitten to the quick, and grabbed hold of Macie's. "I promise."

. . .

MJ had been gone for a full week—and counting. Beyond a brief phone message letting him know she'd landed and a text message telling him that her sister had been discharged and was taking things easy at home, Ross hadn't heard from her. When would she be coming back? *Would* she be coming back? He'd picked up and then set down the fancy red shoe he'd had fixed more times than he cared to count.

An emergency meeting at the station was called, more backlash from the *On Top* blog post come to bite him in the butt. A rival media outlet of southern Christian conservatives had picked up on the story and was exploiting it to steal sponsors. Caught up in coping with the crisis, Ross lost track of time and blew past lunch, but at least being buried kept him from brooding non-stop about MJ, which was a good thing. The next time he looked up, it was almost seven p.m.

Holy cow, Sam! He was supposed to pick her up from play practice—two hours ago. He grabbed for his cell phone. During the meeting, he'd turned the sound setting to silent, then, like lunch, he'd forgotten about it. Four voice mail messages waited, and he'd bet all of them were from Sam.

4:45 p.m.: "Daddy, it's me. Practice ended early. You can come and pick me up anytime. 'Bye."

5:15 p.m.: "Dad, not sure where you are but a couple of kids are going for pizza. Since you're not here yet, I said I'd go. Hope that's cool with you."

5:55 p.m.: "Okay, so I'm back from getting pizza, and I still don't see you anywhere. Sarah Johnson said she'd give me a ride. Guess I'll see you at home."

6:56 p.m.: "This is George Washington University Hospital. There's been a car accident. Your daughter, Samantha Mannon, was transported here by ambulance. She's regained consciousness, and they're working on her in the ER now. Please call as soon as you get this message."

Ross's breath rushed from his body. Shaking, he punched redial but the nurse or doctor or whoever it was who'd called must have done so from an internal line because the call wouldn't connect. *Shit!*

Get a grip, Mannon, and think! He scraped a hand through his hair and for a few seconds focused on simply breathing. The hospital was in the heart of the city in Foggy Bottom. By the time he found the ER direct number and finally got someone on the line, he could be there. That settled it. Grabbing his coat and keys, he raced out.

.

The scenario was one too often repeated among teenagers. Someone from the play practice had gotten hold of some beers, and the cluster of kids parked at the back of the Pizza Hut lot had thrown themselves quite a party. The classmate from whom Sam had accepted the ride was among them. The accident had happened on Rock Creek Parkway at rush hour, the worst possible time. The girl, Sarah, must have nodded off and the car had drifted into the oncoming traffic lane. Sam had reached over to grab the wheel, but it was too late.

Fortunately the driver of the other car had seen them and swerved, avoiding a head-on hit. Still, the car was totaled — not that Ross gave a rat's ass about that.

Sarah had been sent home with minor cuts and bruises and a scary lecture from the police officer assigned to the case. Her license had been confiscated and a court hearing was pending. If Ross were her daddy, the next vehicle she drove would be a donkey cart.

For now, though, all he cared about was Sam. Her injuries were all fixable — a concussion, a broken femur that was going to require surgery, and some pretty dramatic cuts and bruises. Looking up at him from the hospital gurney on which they'd parked her en route to the O.R., she swore, "I didn't drink, Daddy. I didn't even know about the beer. By the time I got there, everybody was inside ordering food. Sarah just seemed giggly and sleepy, but I figured it was because she'd pulled an all-nighter for the history paper we had due. You believe me, right?"

Tears dampened his eyes, tears of self-recrimination and reproach, thanksgiving and gratitude. Not bothering to wipe them away, he reached down to stroke her hair, careful to avoid the gash on her forehead the plastic surgeon had just finished stitching.

"Yes, baby, I do. And I only hope you can forgive me, because I sure won't be forgiving myself anytime soon. Forgetting to pick you up is inexcusable. But that's not for you to fret about. I want you to focus one hundred percent on getting well."

An orderly dressed in scrubs and a see-through plastic cap stepped up to them. "Sir, we have to take her now."

Ross stepped back. "I love you, honey, and I'll be here when you wake up."

"I love you too, Daddy."

Watching them wheel her toward the operating room, he plastered on a smile and waved while his eyes filled with tears. The last time he'd looked on to a similar scene, she'd been about to have her tonsils taken out. Sinking into the plastic waiting room seat, he took a moment to offer up a silent prayer of thanks. It could have gone so very much worse. God, he might have lost her! And just what the hell kind of parent was he? Could there possibly be a bigger hypocrite in all of God's green earth than Ross Mannon? Publicly he preached the importance of putting family first, but in his private life, he'd fallen sadly short of practicing that ideal. What Sam needed was stability, a real home, and maybe, just maybe, that's what Ross needed too. More and more of late, he'd come to associate home with MJ.

Sam's surgery and recovery took just about two hours. They delivered her back to the room, out like a light. Ross held back as the orderlies lifted her from the gurney and laid her on the railed bed.

I'll never let you down again, baby girl. Never!

Minutes melted into hours. Mulling over the future and slugging down black coffee, Ross lost track. At some point the orthopedic surgeon dropped by to run down the surgery—he'd re-aligned the femur bone and inserted a metal plate and screws—and the post-operative treatment plan.

Around 11 p.m., Sam cracked open an eye. "Daddy?"

Ross rushed to her side. "I'm here, baby girl. How're you feeling?"

Her groggy gaze settled briefly on his face. "Pretty…okay. Tired. Thirsty."

He gave her some ice chips, all that she was allowed to have until morning, and she slipped back to sleep.

A night nurse came in to check on her vitals and change out her IV bag, but for the most part they were left alone. A throat being cleared alerted him that their relative peace was about to be broken.

Assuming it must be the nurse again, Ross called out in a high whisper, "She's so peaceful. Can't you let her be a little longer?"

From the doorway, a woman's low voice answered, "I won't wake her, promise."

Ross whipped around. MJ stood on the threshold, a wilted version of the woman he'd dropped off at the airport more than a week ago and yet a sight for sore eyes nonetheless. Even sleep-deprived and makeup free, she was beyond beautiful. Feeling as if he'd wished her there, fearing she might fade away at any minute, he bolted to his feet, nearly spilling the contents of the Styrofoam cup down his shirt.

She shifted her gaze to the bed and whispered, "How's our girl?" He gave the thumb-up sign, and she crept toward the bed. Reaching over the rail, she gently drew up the covers Sam's good leg had kicked off. Looking on, Ross felt his heart turn over and the last of his resistance chip away.

He'd known he had feelings for MJ, strong feelings, but feelings of any degree suddenly seemed far too tepid a descriptor. What he had for MJ was love, honest to goodness love, and as inconvenient as that was and might yet prove to be, he was finally ready to stop fighting it and simply surrender.

She backed up from the bed and turned to him, her gaze still not quite meeting his. Foreboding descended, fisting him in the gut. He set the cup down on the faux wood grain tabletop and signed for her to follow him out into the hallway.

Stepping away from the open door, he filled her in on the details. "Her left leg's pretty busted up—complex fracture of the ankle and a broken femur—but the surgery went great. Once the cast comes off, she'll need some physical therapy, but the orthopedist feels she should heal just fine. Right now the plan is to keep her here for another forty-eight hours and then discharge her."

"That's great news." MJ blew out a breath. "When the doorman told me what had happened, I imagined the worst."

"It almost was worse, a lot worse." He dragged a hand through his hair. "If that other car hadn't seen them in time to swerve, if the passenger side airbag hadn't inflated, she probably wouldn't be here right now."

MJ reached out and laid a hand on his shoulder. "Don't torture yourself. The other driver did see them, the airbag did inflate, and she's here and she's going to be fine."

He nodded. "No thanks to me." He hadn't meant to burden MJ but before he knew it, he was confessing everything, from the silenced cell phone and missed messages to being a no-show at the school pickup. "No wonder she doesn't trust a damn thing I say," he ended miserably.

"That's not true," MJ said firmly.

Switching the subject, he asked, "How's your sister?"

"She's still taking things easy at home and swearing she'll never sneak out again. Here's hoping."

"How are *you*?" Not for the first time since she'd turned up, he noted the dark hollows beneath her eyes. For someone who'd ultimately gotten good news, she still seemed pretty stressed out.

Her gaze shuttered. "I'm okay, happy not to be sitting on a plane for sure. Despite the circumstances, visiting my folks was…cathartic."

Wondering what she meant by that, he said, "You should go get some sleep. You can visit Sam tomorrow when you're both awake."

That she didn't argue further demonstrated that she was dragging on her feet. "Okay, if you're sure." She turned to go.

He started after her. "Hold up, I'm driving you."

Looking back, she waved him off. "Thanks, but I'm a big girl and a New Yorker. I take cabs all the time. In fact, I took one here."

That might be, but Ross wasn't budging. "It's almost one in the morning and this isn't New York. My car's right here in the hospital garage. You'll be doing me a favor. I could stand getting out of here for a while."

She hesitated for a few seconds before giving way. "Okay, if you're sure."

"I am."

Walking with him to the elevator bank, she remarked, "You look like you could use some sleep yourself."

He snorted. "Other than feeling like the worst parent on the planet, I'm raring to go."

She reached over and laid a hand on his forearm, the shirtsleeve rolled up to his elbow. Now that his parental panic had subsided, her fingers on his flesh set off a trail of tingling.

"Ross, how many times must I say this? It wasn't your fault."

"Bull crap, it was entirely my fault. The whole reason she was in that car was because I missed picking her up. I left my own kid stranded and at the mercy of a drunk driver. Father of the Year, I'm not."

The elevator doors opened. He held back for her to enter, and then stepped inside, hesitating over which garage floor to push. When he'd parked, he'd been half crazed, not knowing how badly Sam was hurt. Digging into his pants pocket, he found his parking stub and pulled it out. The second level, he remembered now. He punched the button for two and the elevator began its descent.

The doors opened again, and they stepped out. The garage, which had been filled almost to capacity when he'd arrived, was nearly deserted, making his Ford Explorer easy to find. He pulled out his keys, clicked the unlock button, and opened the passenger's side door.

Macie slid inside and he crossed to the driver's side and climbed in. Locking the doors, he tossed the keys in the beverage cup holder and turned to her.

A worried look settled over her face. "You're exhausted. Are you sure you're okay to drive?"

He nodded. "I've had enough coffee to float a battleship. Right now, I couldn't fall asleep if I tried." That was suddenly a good thing because as far as he was concerned, they had some serious talking to do and a whole heap of air to clear. "Truth is, I'm not much interested in talking about me anymore right now. I'd rather talk about what's up with you."

Her gaze slid away. "What do you mean?"

He blew out a heavy breath. "You're keeping something from me, something big. What is it?"

She firmed her mouth as though afraid some secret might spill out. "Nothing you or anyone else can do anything about."

"Why not try me? I'd like to help if I can."

She looked up—eye contact at last! "If I could time travel back by a month and change things, I would, but I can't. None of us can redo our past."

"Who's asking you to?" Wondering exactly what she was regretting—coming to DC, accepting the job, accepting... him?—he said, "Let's talk about the here-and-now, starting with whether or not you're back to stay?"

She dropped her gaze to the folded hands in her lap. "I'm back for now but...you should probably start searching for my replacement."

Her response didn't really surprise him. She'd said more or less what he'd expected—dreaded—hearing from the moment she'd set foot inside Sam's hospital room. Still, hearing the actual words sent his heart sinking deeper than a

Texas oil well.

He reached over and gently cupped her cheek. "You are one hundred percent absolutely irreplaceable, not only to Sam but to me. After everything we've all just been through, how can you still not know that?"

Her anguished face slashed at his heart. "Ross, please."

He reached down and clasped her cold hands between his. Chafing her chilly fingers, he said, "Look, MJ, I know things between us were stuck in limbo when you left, and that was mostly—okay entirely—my fault. But—"

She cut him off with a fierce shake of her head. "Stop apologizing! It's not you, it's me. I'm the one who's messed up and if I didn't get that already, this past week more than drove it home." Her voice broke. "I hadn't been home in almost two years, and it took my kid sister nearly overdosing to get me there. I need to spend some serious time reevaluating my life and where it's going—or *not* going."

Ross tried not to sound as hurt as he suddenly felt. "What about Sam and me? I'd like to think we're more than a pit stop."

"Of course you are. I've come to…care for you both… deeply."

It wasn't exactly a declaration of love, but for now Ross would take what he could get. He'd missed her so much that instead of pressing for more answers, he found himself pressing her against him. His lips found her forehead, her closed eyelids, and finally her mouth and suddenly they were making out like teenagers, his hands inside her pants, her hands pulling at his shirt.

Rather than repeat history, he tore himself away and shoved the key in the ignition. "If it's all the same to you, I'd rather our first time wasn't in a car." MJ deserved better, the very best, from him and if their courtship so far hadn't exactly been by the book—they'd been skipping whole chapters right and left—the least he could do was provide a proper bed.

Her puzzled gaze flew to his. "What about Sam?"

"Earlier she woke up for about two minutes. With the anesthesia from the surgery and now the pain meds they're pumping into her, I expect she'll be knocked out for the rest of the night. I'll come back first thing in the morning. Right now, I'm taking you home to bed—*my* bed. Assuming no objections, I'm fixing to make love to you the old-fashioned way—slow, thorough, and all through the night."

Chapter Nine

The condo door had barely closed behind them when Macie tore off her coat and started on the buttons of her blouse. A while ago in the garage she'd been able to relax and let herself go, probably because she'd known Ross was too much of a gentleman to take her in his car. But now that they were in his home and about to really go to bed together, the old fears fought their way to the surface. Suddenly she was sixteen, not twenty-six, crushed in a stifling embrace and choking on cheap cologne.

Ross laid his hand over hers. "Hey, slow down, we're not in any race. Besides, I was looking forward to doing that."

"Sorry, just trying to get to the main event." She gulped down more air and looked beyond him to the kitchen. "Maybe we should have a drink." Pulse pounding, she couldn't remember if there was any vodka left.

He stared at her. "You want a cocktail now? It's almost two in the morning."

She let out a scratchy laugh. "I'm sure it's five o'clock somewhere."

If she couldn't be numb, she'd have to go back to being

fast, otherwise the anxiety would paralyze her. She launched herself at his chest, her clumsy cold fingers plucking at his shirt buttons.

He wrapped a hand about her wrists and lowered her arms to her sides, his gaze searching hers. "Who hurt you, MJ? It's obvious that being on the receiving end of a man's touch makes you antsy as a cat in a roomful of rocking chairs."

She shook her head, hating that after all these years she was still so see-through, so broken. "That's ridiculous. Before I came here, I had a boyfriend back in New York, a *serious* boyfriend." God, she sounded so sixteen.

Not to mention that she was lying—again. Zach had been fun to be around when he was in one of his good moods, but if she were honest with herself, what he'd mostly been was convenient. He'd never come close to "complete package" status. Still, she'd stuck it out, not because she was a masochist, at least not especially, but because she hadn't been any closer to committing to a real relationship than he had.

"You have this problem with him, too?"

How she hated feeling vulnerable. "Tex, I have zero problems with sex—and moves you haven't even heard of."

Fuck MJ—Macie Graham was out of the closet with a vengeance, and she had something to prove. She settled her palm over his fly. Behind the zipper of his khakis was a hard-on the size of…Texas. She cupped the firm flesh and predictably his eyes flew open.

Still, he blew out a breath and moved her hand away. "Hold onto that thought. For now, let's you and I sit down on that sofa over there and have us a talk."

He held out his hand. Macie hesitated.

"Come on, honey."

His gentleness undid her. On the brink of tears, she took his hand and let him guide her into the great room.

They sat side-by-side on the sectional sofa. Yanking the ends of her blouse together, she drew her locked knees up to her waist. "I'm sorry I messed up." A breath shuddered out of her. She suddenly felt empty and cold.

"You didn't mess up anything." Ross wrapped a steadying arm about her shoulders and she leaned into him. "Just breathe, okay?" He demonstrated, drawing a deep breath and then exhaling.

Macie followed. Amazingly it helped. "You're...good at this...breathing thing."

He cracked a smile. "If radio host doesn't work out for me, I figure Lamaze coach can be my fallback."

Improbably, she laughed. Her deadlock on her blouse loosened and he reached around her. "Here, let's get you put back together for now. You okay with that?"

She nodded, and he started doing up her blouse buttons. "First cooking and now putting clothes back on otherwise willing women," she mused aloud. "You're blowing your macho image big time."

Looking up, he winked. "We'll keep it our secret."

Secrets—Macie knew all about them. Sitting back, she admitted, "I'm broken, Ross. I can't...I've never been able to, you know...*come*."

He sent her a concerned look. "You talk to a doctor about this?"

"The problem's not physical, it's...mental." She gathered a long, deep breath. "When I was a teenager about Sam's age, my pastor molested me."

There, she'd said it.

He slipped an arm back around her. "Baby, I'm so sorry."

She nodded. "When I finally found the courage to tell my mother, she wouldn't believe me. Pastor Meeks was a good, God-fearing man in her eyes and the community's, which meant I must be making it all up."

Macie had fought back the only way she knew how, coloring her hair every shade of the rainbow, wearing all black, and cutting classes to hide out in the woods bordering the football field. There, she'd spent the better part of her schooldays smoking weed and reading Sylvia Plath and wondering when being alive would stop hurting so much.

"My school guidance counselor saw something was wrong, everyone did—my grades had fallen from A's to C's and lower—but I never told anyone again. All I wanted was to forget, forget and be numb. I started drinking and using drugs. Mostly pot but I tried pills, too." She looked up sharply. "I never exactly bottomed out, but I never really rose above the experience either." She paused and looked over at him. "During this visit, my mother actually apologized. So did my dad. I can't tell you how huge that was. *Sorry* isn't in my parents' regular vocabulary. I'd always figured that if that ever happened, it would be like someone flicking a magic wand in my face. I wouldn't be only vindicated. I'd suddenly be all better, all...healed." Her shoulders fell. She sighed. "Obviously that's not the case."

Throughout, he'd let her go on uninterrupted. Now he asked, "Have you thought about talking to someone, a professional?"

She nodded. "I did once, a few years ago." She'd just started dating Zach, who'd complained she was cold in bed. The fear of losing him, the first real "boyfriend" she'd had in years, had prompted her to seek help.

"What did he say?"

In spite of the sober circumstances, she smiled. "It was a *she* actually, not a shrink but a gynecologist. After the exam, we talked in her office about post traumatic stress disorder, and she gave me a referral to a support group for sexual assault survivors." Only taking a seat in the group's mandatory circle, Macie hadn't felt like a survivor at all but a member of the walking dead. "I went once, which was one time too many. It sucked. Sitting in a circle of sad-eyed women all scared of their own shadows wasn't my thing then or now. I like to keep my pity parties as solo events." She tried for a laugh but he didn't join her.

"Ever think about trying a different group or a private therapist, maybe both?"

"I take the brochure out every few months and look at it. Does that count?"

"Probably not."

She fingered the fringe of the throw pillow she'd somehow ended up hugging. "Every time I go to bed with a man I try telling myself it can be different…only it never is." Shit, she probably shouldn't have told him *that*. Assault survivor or not, Martha Jane Gray would be celibate. Macie Graham was definitely not.

She glanced up to gauge his reaction. The compassion in his eyes almost undid her. "Maybe you've never been with the right man."

Macie looked away to the far wall, where a framed black-and-white photograph of the Washington Monument hung — pretty phallic imagery now that she thought about it — and shook her head. "And I suppose you're the man for the job?"

His hand curved around her shoulder. His other one played with her ponytail; the latter was unexpectedly soothing. "Would it be so terrible if I was?"

She snorted. "I'd just as soon skip the macho routine if it's all the same to you. I'm sure you're good — okay, *very* good — but I don't think we're a good idea. I'm just not — "

He stopped her with his kiss, brushing his mouth over her still moving lips. Macie felt the warm tingle trickle through her all the way down to her toes. Pulling back, he rested his forehead against hers. "Hush up and listen. It's going to be different this time because I'm me and you're you. And we're going to take this thing between us, whatever it is, just as slow as you need, got it?"

She nodded.

"And the single solitary second I do something that makes you uncomfortable—or scared—you're going to tell me. And then I'm going to stop." His hand fell away. He winked at her and the sudden "all better" feeling put pixie dust to shame.

She nodded, the held-back tears choking off any hope she'd had of answering.

"And by the way, seeing as I'm from the 'old school' as you put it, I don't hold with all this modern woman stiff upper lip crap. If you need to cry, you cry. Okay?"

"O-okay."

The next thing she knew, she was sobbing into his chest while he held her, and pressed kisses into her hair and her wet cheeks, and whispered for her not to fret herself but to let it all out. Because he was here and maybe, finally, everything was going to be all right.

She cried as she hadn't cried in years, until she didn't have any more tears or breath or sadness to spend. She cried until the hurt and the anger both faded to a manageable sting, crowded out by the cozy contentment she felt enveloping a very private part of her. She cried until she lost track of what she was crying about—loss of innocence, betrayal by the grownups who were supposed to have loved and protected her, or maybe just the beautiful cleansing release of finally, *finally* letting it all go.

At some point, Ross rose, picked her up, and carried her down the hallway and into his bedroom. Coming up on the bed, he lowered her gently onto the mattress and climbed in beside her. Half asleep, Macie snuggled against him. He pressed kisses onto her damp cheek, whispering assurances that she was safe, he was there, and from here on everything was going to be fine, just fine. Eyes closed, Macie let herself drift off.

She was safe. Ross was here.

But for how long?

⋅

Macie awoke to Hank Williams's "Your Cheatin' Heart," not the custom ringtone she would have ever selected for an alarm. Keeping her eyes closed, she willed the stubborn sound to cease. When it didn't, she reached over to the night table, hoping to hit snooze.

Only she wasn't in her bedroom, not the one back in New York, not the one in DC, either. She was in Ross's room—and the space beside her was empty. Remembering everything that had gone down the night before, she covered her hands over her face and groaned.

A cough drew her attention to the door. She cracked open an eye and lifted her head from the pillow. Ross stood on the threshold, wearing a T-shirt, jeans, and a pillow crease on one cheek. Reflexively she reached for the sheet, and then saw that she still wore her clothes.

He entered, carrying his signature cup of coffee. "Sleep okay?"

"I did." She shifted over to make room for him on the side of the bed. "What time is it?"

"It's after noon." He handed her the coffee, then reached around her to hit "dismiss" on the cell phone.

"What about Sam?" She remembered that he'd meant to go back to the hospital that morning.

He handed her the mug. "I went in early this morning and helped her with breakfast, then came home and crawled back into bed with a certain sleepyhead."

Macie took a sip of coffee, savoring the strong chicory flavor. Just a few weeks ago it would have been too potent for her liking, but now she couldn't imagine having it any other way. "About last night..." She set the cup down on the nightstand, making sure the bottom met the coaster so as not to leave a ring on the wood—talk about changed. "I'm sorry for being such a disappointment."

He propped a hip against the side of the bed. "Did I say I was disappointed?"

Chivalry was one thing but his sense of honor was way over the top. "Ross, we didn't—"

"Look here, honey, what you went through was horrific, a crime in every way. For what it's worth, I spent a good part of the night thinking up ways to track down that sick little asshole."

Touched, Macie shook her head. "The statute of limitations ran out a long time ago and even if it hadn't, he's an old man now. If he's even still alive, he's hopefully too decrepit to ever hurt another child. It's time I moved on. I *want* to move on, Ross, starting with a redo of last night." She reached out to him. "Do you still want me?"

He swallowed hard, the residual ripple traveling down the muscled column of his throat. "I want you so damned much it scares me."

Wrapping her hand around his wrist, she drew his hand down. "Let's make a new deal—no more being scared for either of us."

He came down beside her. "Just so you know, I'm not letting you out of this bed until you come."

She smiled. "Why Dr. Mannon, that sounds like a

challenge."

A Texas-size grin spread across his face. "Darlin', you can take it anyway you like, but above all—consider it a promise."

●

Lying on her stomach, Macie lifted her head from the pillow to look back at Ross rubbing her back. "This is absolute decadence. I could lie here like this all day."

He chuckled. "I'm not stopping you."

He'd taken off his T-shirt but kept on his jeans. A lock of hair fell over his forehead, making him look like a boy, the sight filling her with tenderness.

"But your arms must be getting tired," she protested.

He shook his head. "Not hardly. I could do this for hours."

Macie didn't doubt it. Her Texas gentleman was the most patient man she'd ever known—and the most giving. They'd been in bed together for more than an hour and still they hadn't come close to having sex. Earlier she'd tried to give him a blowjob but he'd refused, insisting this day was all about her.

"Tomorrow when I go to pick Sam up from the hospital, we'll both turn back into pumpkins, so enjoy it while it lasts."

Macie stared. "Sam! I was supposed to visit her today."

Gentle hands urged her back down on the mattress. "I told her you were back but feeling under the weather—not exactly a lie."

Macie bit her lip, thinking of all the lies she'd so far told both Ross and Sam.

His hand on her spine traveled lower still, stroking the curve where her back and buttocks met. "How are you feeling now?" The press of his lips on her lower back followed the question, and relaxation took a sudden, erotic turn.

Macie sucked down a breath. "Better."

His next kiss fell on her left buttock cheek. "And how about now?"

"Pretty...amazing."

He kissed her right cheek as well, shaping it with his hand. "And now?"

"Ross, you are *killing* me."

"Good. Now touch yourself for me."

"What?"

"You heard me. Reach around and touch yourself. I'll be right here."

Was he really suggesting that she masturbate in front of him? Given his conservative social values, she'd assumed any sex they had would be missionary style, totally vanilla. So far they hadn't done much more than make out and already the vanilla was turning into a swirl cone.

He came down lightly atop her. Coarse chest hair brushed her back. Shifting onto his side, he drew her against him. His hardness pressed against her, not terribly far away from the spots he'd branded with his kisses.

"Don't you want to put on a condom and—"

He cut her off with a cluck of his tongue. "You're always in such a hurry. We have the rest of the day and night. I'm not going anywhere and neither are you. Now touch yourself, darlin'. Let's see how good you can feel."

She hesitated and then slipped a hand between her parted thighs. She was wet, really wet—a good sign. She'd masturbated in private plenty of times—any woman who claimed she didn't must be a saint or a monumental liar. Sometimes she even managed to stir a tepid tingling. Nice as that felt, it fell sadly short of the orgasmic pleasure she'd researched and written about in articles over the last five years. Doing so had made her feel like a fraud.

As if reading her mind, he whispered, "Don't make it

about reaching some finish line. Enjoy getting there."

He bit the side of her neck, and Macie shuddered. "I'll try."

He covered her hand with his, not guiding but going along with the motion she set. "That's it, baby. Don't hold back. Take it all."

Pressing back against him, she slipped a finger inside herself, imagining it was him entering her.

His hot whisper struck the shell of her ear. "You're so wet. And hot."

She swallowed hard. "It's you who's making me this way." Wet and throbbing, her clit beat like a miniature heart.

"I can't wait to kiss you there, to taste you."

The image of his blond head bent to her spread thighs sent the sensation skyrocketing. Holding onto the scenario, she circled her clitoris and the pleasure peaked.

"That's it. Slow and steady wins the race."

That might be true, but suddenly Macie couldn't hold back any longer, not because she was afraid anxiety might take over but because she was so aroused she thought she might burst. Like a bud about to break into bloom, her clit felt hard and hot and tight. She circled herself again, firmer and faster.

And suddenly it happened. The tension uncoiled, the shackles fell away. Spasms wracked her. Pleasure filled her, not just between her legs but everywhere, her whole being, a precious, long overdue gift.

And throughout it all was Ross, his arms anchoring her, his warmth enveloping her. Knowing she was finally safe, she threw back her head and called out the single word that summed up all that made sense in her newly discovered universe.

"Ross!"

The fairy-tale fervor ended far too fast, leaving her limp and spent and satisfied, at least for the time being. Breathing hard, she shifted to look at her personal Prince Charming.

He greeted her with a big grin and shining eyes. "Welcome to the club, darlin'."

Rolling onto her back, she reached for the sheet. "Does this mean I'm accepted as a member?"

Lifting up on one elbow, he grinned down at her. "Yes ma'am, card-carrying and in good standing."

She glanced at the clock. It was nearing five p.m. How had that happened? "Hungry?" she asked, suddenly aware that she hadn't eaten since the airline dinner the previous day.

"Starved." He leaned in to nip her neck.

Macie smiled. "Great, because I know someone who makes a mean plate of huevos rancheros."

Ross grinned. "So long as the chef cooks naked, I'm all in."

•

They ate their eggs in bed, washed down with a bottle of chianti they'd been fortunate to find in the back of the pantry closet. Macie had known sex could be hot, but before now she'd never known it could be playful, too. Ross sipped hot sauce from the well of her navel. He fed her dollops of sour cream from his fork and his fingers. He trailed spicy kisses from her mouth down to her belly and beyond. When he slid his hands to her inner thighs, Macie let her legs fall open with a sigh. When he found her with his mouth, she closed her eyes and gave herself over to his tender lips and laving tongue. And finally when he left her just long enough to reach over, open his nightstand drawer, and take out a foil wrapped condom, she watched him without anxiety, only eagerness.

"Don't you think you've worn those jeans long enough?" As awesome as his ass looked in the comfortably worn denim, she'd bet her last buck it would look even more awesome wearing nothing at all.

Sitting back on his heels, he tore open the condom wrapper, his gaze never leaving her face. "You tell me."

"I'd say so." She sat up, knelt, and slowly, lovingly drew his zipper down.

His erection spilled free, a velvety hard heat that pooled into her palm. Macie's mouth watered. Her clit throbbed. She stroked her fingers along the length of him, loving the way he couldn't seem to take his eyes off her, that big and strong though he was, she had the power to make him tremble. A bead of moisture dropped into her palm like a liquid jewel. Wanting, *needing*, to see and touch and taste the rest of him, Macie grabbed the waist of his jeans and started tugging them down and off. Ross helped her. Kicking free of the pants, he turned back to her. Narrow hips, powerful thighs, and a runner's muscled calves matched the magnificence of his erection. Macie sucked in a breath. He was, in a word, stunning.

She reached for him, her fingers sinking into the sleek, firm flesh of his buttocks as she pulled him closer. "Professor, in case no one's told you before, you have .one bodacious butt," she said, forgetting all about being "Martha Jane" in the joy of being herself.

Chuckling, Ross rolled on the condom. "Given that I spend most of my days sitting on it, I don't get a lot of… positive feedback, but thanks." Sheathed, he settled his gaze on hers. "Slow and steady," he said. "And in case you're wondering, I'll do anything you want."

Macie swallowed hard. "*Anything*?" So much for her earlier assumptions that he'd be conservative sexually.

Anything encompassed…a hell of a lot.

A slow smile spread across his face. "Yes, ma'am." He lay down on his back, pulled the pillow under his head, and waited.

Still kneeling, Macie hesitated. "What are you doing?"

He grinned up at her, though the tautness about his mouth hinted at what the restraint cost him. "Giving you your chance to be a modern woman."

Macie was already aroused, but the sudden reality of having more than six feet three inches of firm Texas male stretched out and available for her exclusive pleasure carried her almost to climax.

"Whatever you say, Tex." She lifted one leg, threw it over him, and boldly settled herself atop. Bracing a hand on the pillow by his head, she reached down with her other hand and fitted him to her. There was no doubt about it. He was huge. Fortunately she was ready. More than ready—she couldn't wait. And she no longer had to.

Holding his gaze, she shifted, filling herself with him in one exquisite, perfectly penetrating thrust. "Oh…my…God."

Fuller than she'd ever felt before, Macie hesitated but only a moment. Bracing a fisted hand on either side of Ross's head, she began to move, back and forth, up and down.

Ross's steadying hands anchored to her hips. The same blunt fingers that had stoked her somnolent sex to life now imprinted deliciously on her skin. "That's it, take what you need, darlin'. Better yet, take what you *want*."

Macie picked up pace, grinding greedily against him. Likely she'd be sore tomorrow but, as a certain fictional Southern belle had famously pointed out, tomorrow was another day. Presently all that existed was the here and now with Ross.

The pressure inside her built. Her nipples beaded, her clit

buzzed. Perspiration filmed her forehead and the backs of her knees. The muscles of her thighs quivered with exhaustion. Her arms ached and her fisted hands began to feel bruised. It was pure torture—and it felt so purely good.

She pulled back and pushed him into her once more. As she did, their gazes met, melded. It was, she realized, the first time she'd ever made love while meeting a man's eyes. In the past, she'd always looked away, sending herself on a mental mini-break until she was done. But mindless sex didn't interest her now. It hadn't much interested her then. Still, it took being with Ross to realize just how very much she'd missed. He was the "complete package," all the dancing, dragon slaying Disney princes rolled into one. Being here in his bed brought every fevered fairy-tale fantasy she'd ever harbored to brilliant, blazing life.

A gritty groan escaped him. His grip on her tightened. He bucked his hips, driving deeply into her. The first spasm struck hard, taking her totally unaware. The second sent her clenching, the current of sensation traveling to her toes.

"Ross, I've never—" Before she could finish, Macie shuddered around him, her tremors milking his manhood, triggering his release.

She caught a flash of blue fire as his eyes flew open. "Oh, Christ, MJ!"

Spent, she collapsed onto him. His arms banded about her, keeping her from falling. His one big hand slid down her damp back to shape her buttocks, as though marking her as his. Macie relaxed against him, even now amazed at how beautifully their bodies fit, at how absolutely right it felt to lie prone atop him, his penis still inside her.

A tear trailed her cheek, a happy one this time. She'd waited a decade to be free of the past. Thanks to Ross, she finally was.

• • •

Ross woke up the next morning feeling like a changed man. With MJ at his side, he felt like he could conquer just about anything, including getting Sam whatever help she needed. Looking at her curled up beside him, the realization hit him anew.

I *love this woman, I purely love her.*

He didn't want a fling with her or a relationship where they saw each other on weekends and maybe one weeknight. He wanted her in his life twenty-four-seven, for holidays and regular days, the good times and bad. He wanted her as his wife forever and for always.

He'd wait until they brought Sam home from the hospital and then he'd propose. Once she accepted—and after last night he felt pretty sure she would—they'd order in pizza and celebrate.

Like a family.

• • •

They got Sam home by lunchtime. She insisted on sitting up and eating at the table but afterward she was happy to settle into her room for a rest.

Ross looked down at the sandwich he'd barely touched. "I never was good at this stuff but suddenly I feel rustier than an old nail," he muttered.

Macie cast her gaze around. Making sure they were alone, she dropped her voice and said, "Funny, I don't recall any creaking last night." She flashed him a smile and leaned over to kiss the tip of his nose.

"I'm serious, honey, I have something to say to you." He pushed back his chair and stood.

Wondering if he might be regretting going to bed with her, she froze. "W-what is it?"

To her shock, he went down on one knee. "Martha Jane Gray, will you do me the honor of marrying me?"

Stunned, Macie stared down at him. "You're proposing!"

He grinned up at her. "I'm sure giving it my best shot."

"But, Ross, you don't even know me, not really."

"Darlin', I know you're sweet and smart and funny and as good-hearted as they come. You're everything I want in a wife and a second mother to Sam." He reached up for her hand. "Hell, I was starting to doubt women like you existed anymore."

Staring down, Macie blinked away tears, but they weren't happy ones. A man was finally ready to commit to her—only the woman he wanted wasn't real but a persona she'd put on along with her pale pink lipstick and pastel wardrobe. She swallowed hard, feeling as if the lies she'd spent the last weeks spinning were suddenly being pulled over her, a tight, dense web from which there was no escape. She was everything he wanted in a woman, in a wife.

Only everything about her was a lie.

She bolted from her chair, her body and brain shifting into survival mode. "You think you know me, but you don't."

He stood stiffly, wincing as, no doubt, the old football injury kicked in. "Of course I know you." His smugness made her want to hit him.

Instead, she said, "Really, then let's play a little game—truth or dare. Only the dare is all on your side, mister. Want to know what political party I'm registered to? Go ahead and ask me—I dare you."

Ross stared at her. "Don't tell me you're a—"

"A Democrat, yep, sure am. A *Liberal* Democrat and a proud member of NOW. And for your information, all those wholesome, home-cooked meals from the past weeks—other than the eggs, I didn't make any of them."

After weeks of hiding her true self, or at least some pretty major parts of it, it felt good to debunk the lies. Even if doing so might mean driving him away, she couldn't keep up the façade. Not after last night.

Ross's mouth hung at half-mast. "Then how—"

"My friend Stefanie owns a personal chef service and business is booming. It seems that here in Washington, DC, most women have better things to do than slave away in the kitchen."

His gaze narrowed. "She keep house, too?"

"No, but she hooked me up with a really great maid service."

"You hire a chauffeur to drive Sam?"

"No, I actually did that myself, along with picking up your dry cleaning and doing your laundry and helping your daughter with her homework—just a few of the hundred or so tasks involved in running a household."

Their raised voices must have reached Sam in her room. Hobbling in, she looked between them and asked, "What's going on? Why are you fighting?"

Ross answered for them both. "We'll talk later. For now, I need you to go back to your room."

Macie shot him a look. Did he really think he could warehouse his daughter in her room whenever life got too real or too messy? To Sam, she said, "Your father and I are just having a discussion."

Sam rolled her eyes. "A discussion, give me a break. I remember he and Mom used to have a lot of those when I was a little kid."

Ross scowled. "For your information, young lady, you still qualify as a kid. A kid who's going to spend all of next weekend locked up inside here tighter than San Quentin unless she gets her butt in her room pronto."

Watching Sam hold her ground, Macie was silently, secretly proud of her. Sam tightened her fingers on the crutch's crossbar and straightened her back. "That's right, Dad. Go ahead and shut me out, just like you do to everyone who doesn't see things your way."

For a moment Ross stood stock still. Then, as if suddenly recovering himself, he said, "Then stay. MJ and I have just been *discussing* how all these fine suppers she's been serving were catered and how the apartment's in such great shape because she hired a housecleaning service. You know about any of that?"

Sam darted a look to Macie and the sick feeling in her stomach spread. "Maybe."

He looked hard at Sam. "I asked you a straight-up question, young lady, and I expect a straight-up answer."

Poor Sam, Ross was really grilling her. Looking on, Macie had to hold back from rushing over to hug her.

"I didn't know for certain but I suspected…stuff," Sam said. "She served up such big dinners but until lately I never really saw her cook anything. And she seemed real protective of the trash. But what's the big deal? It all got done."

Ross squared his shoulders. "The big deal is that I don't much like being lied to." He swung his gaze back to Macie. Her face felt flushed, as if she'd spent a day baking sans sunscreen on the beach.

"I didn't lie," Sam insisted, her cheeks turning bright. "I just didn't tell. That's different."

Eyes on Macie, he said, "That is just the sort of moral relativism I would expect from someone like—"

"Like me?" That did it! Until now, she'd held back, but going forward the gloves would be off. "If you mean someone who'd dare to want more from life than to be at the beck and call of some beer guzzling man sprawled on the couch in front of the TV, then yes, guilty as charged."

Come to think of it, she couldn't remember ever seeing Ross drink a beer while watching TV. Other than *Blue Bloods* and *Law and Order* and the black-and-white movies they showed on the Turner Classics channel, he always said most of the programs on TV were crap, but that wasn't really the point. It was his *attitude* that she objected to, not any specific action.

Frustrated to the point of throwing things, she ran a hand through her hair, wrecking the rest of the ponytail and popping a hairpin out of place. "Sam, sweetie, your father's right. You shouldn't have to be a part of this."

Sam hesitated and then nodded. "Okay, I get it. You're unlawfully imprisoning me in my room. If anyone needs me, that's where I'll be."

• • •

Ross looked from MJ to his daughter and then back, thinking that any man who thought he knew a damned thing about women had better think again.

He waited for the sound of Sam's door closing before starting in. "Well, Miss Gray, it looks like you've made a liar out of my daughter and a fool out of me, but I guess that's all in a day's work for a woman like you. Begging your pardon, I should have said *Ms.* Gray out of respect to your feminist sensitivities and such."

MJ shot him a daggered look. "Not sensitivities, Ross, values. Yes, *values*. The trouble is we just don't share the same ones."

"Then why come to work for me?"

She hesitated. "Because...I needed a...change of scene from New York."

She was lying. This time at least he could tell without any trouble. "Let me guess, joining the Christian missionary family in Belize didn't much appeal?"

Her gaze shuttered. "You could say that."

"That degree from CUA, you fake it, too?"

"No, it's real. Liberals can like kids, too."

"Your feelings for Sam, was that all part of the act?"

MJ shook her head. "Of course not, I honestly really... like Sam. Actually, I'm crazy about her."

He folded his arms across his chest. "Like you're crazy about old movies and huevos rancheros?"

She lifted her chin. "I've always loved old movies. I'd never had spicy eggs before I met you but now that I have, I really like them and...I really liked making them for you last night."

Ross swallowed hard. She'd cooked wearing an old apron they'd found at the bottom of a kitchen drawer—and nothing else. But already last night seemed like a faraway time and place, a dream. Not a dream—a fairy tale. Only minus the happy ending.

"That story about how your kid sister nicknamed you MJ, is that even true?" Ever since that night they'd stood together on the Kennedy Center terrace and shared their first kiss, she'd been MJ to him. He felt like the funny little nickname was engraved on his heart. If that turned out to be a lie, too, he wasn't rightly sure what he would do.

Tears spangled her lower lashes. "It's true, it's all true. The things that really matter are all true. They're all me—the *real* me."

"There are two of you and only one of me. So, sorry Martha Jane or MJ or whatever name the *real* you is going by today, but you'll have to excuse me. I'm having trouble keeping up." Too angry and overwhelmed to know what to believe, he whipped away.

"Where are you going?" she demanded as if she still had any rights over him, as if anything he said or did from here on was any of her goddamn business.

Setting his course for his bedroom to change, he answered anyway. "Where I go whenever I need to keep from doing something that'll come back to bite me in the butt: Rock Creek Park for a run."

Chapter Ten

Pounding the path into powder, Ross ran his customary five miles—and kept going. Jesus H. Christ, to think he'd actually proposed marriage to a card-carrying member of NOW! He must be a seriously bad judge of character, a bad judge of women, or maybe both. From here on he would devote all his energies to straightening out his kid. He couldn't afford to have his emotions tangled up with a woman who'd admitted to lying to him from the start.

Two hours later, he returned to the apartment, sopping with sweat and bad knee aching. Eerie quiet greeted him— the cold shoulder routine again?

He headed for Sam's room to check on her. Limping out into the living room, she saved him the time. "Oh, Daddy!"

Taking in her stricken face and streaming eyes he hurried over, too concerned to care that he must be tracking mud on the beige carpet.

Reaching her, he slung a sweaty arm around her shuddering shoulders. "Sam, honey, what happened? Is your leg hurting? You take your pain medicine?"

She swung her head from side-to-side. "She…left."

It took him several seconds to absorb the news. "MJ left?" Even though he'd planned on telling her to go, the preemptive strike landed like a fist in his gut.

Between halting breaths, Sam managed to get out that MJ had packed her bags after he'd left and called for a cab to the train station.

It was one thing to break his heart but breaking his kid's was another matter entirely. "Heartless—"

"No, Daddy, it wasn't like that. She was crying pretty bad, even worse than me, and she kept hugging me and telling me that she'd never forget me, that even though she couldn't stay, we were friends for life."

Ross broke away and rushed to MJ's room. The closet was cleared out, the suitcase gone. Set out atop the dresser, one red-velvet slipper anchored a note. Weak kneed, he pulled out the folded slip of stationery.

Ross,

You asked me earlier "why"? Well, trust me on this one, going into all the gory details would be pointless and painful for everyone. Let's just say I'm not the person you thought I was, and it's better for all of us that I leave now. Please give my love to Sam and tell her to forget what I said about fairy tales. After her cast comes off and she finishes the therapy, I want her to put on these shoes, knock her heels together three times—and believe in Happily Ever After every chance she gets.

MJ.

P.S. I may not be the princess perfect person you thought I was, but thanks for helping me remember the

PERSON I STARTED OUT WANTING TO BE.

• • •

Macie spent the train ride back to New York conducting an in-depth interview—with herself. The bottom line was she didn't much like what she saw. The never-ending search for the next sensational storyline had consumed her for five years. Now that struck her as pointless and sad.

Later, walking in the West Village, the colorfully lit Empire State Building a beacon in the near distance, it occurred to her that before she'd met Ross, her life had been as monochromatic as her all-black wardrobe. Now that she'd let in the light, the love, she couldn't go back to the way things were before. More to the point, she didn't want to. Maybe it was time to revisit her dream of working for a small environmental magazine. The grassroots pay scale wouldn't support staying on in New York, but leaving the bright lights and big city no longer seemed like such a tragedy. The past weeks had changed her profoundly and forever. Though it could never work out between her and Ross, though her heart was hurting more than she'd ever imagined a heart could hurt, still she'd realized one very valuable thing.

It was time to move on.

• • •

Ross arranged a week's leave, prerecorded his program, and then put himself and Sam on a plane to Paris, Texas. The three-hour flight into Dallas Fort Worth and the two-hour car drive to Paris provided plenty of opportunity for self-reflection. Why had he gone to graduate school in the first place? The answer wasn't long in coming but the simplicity all but knocked him to his knees. *I wanted to make a difference.*

The research had engaged his mind but what he'd really loved about being a college professor was teaching. Somehow he'd gotten sidetracked, caught up first in academia's publish-or-perish culture and later the sudden, head spinning sensation of instant celebrity. Being a nationally known talking head was a monumental ego trip, not to mention just about the best substitute he could find for the real life he was missing out on. Sure, hundreds of thousands of people knew his name, but how many knew the real him?

Before MJ had blown into his life like a twister, shaking things up, shaking *him* up, he hadn't even known his own daughter, not really. It was high time he did what he was always telling other people to do—go back to basics. High time for Ross Mannon to sign off as morals arbiter for the whole world and put his own sorry-ass life back in order.

That evening, as he helped Sam up onto his parents' front porch, he wondered why he'd ever left.

Wearing her apron, his mother rushed out to greet them. Careful of the crutches, she enveloped Sam in a hug. "Samantha, you've got so grown up. How you feeling, honey?"

"Pretty good, Grandma. The cast itches."

Ross added, "It comes off in five weeks, and then she'll start physical therapy and wear an immobilizer for a while. Once the break heals, her leg should be as good as new."

His mother let out a relieved breath. "Thank the good Lord for that. For now, though, she should rest." Turning back to Sam, she said, "I put you in the downstairs bedroom so you wouldn't have to worry with the stairs. Go on in and I'll bring you some pie in a bit."

"Thanks, Grandma."

His mother's arms went around him next. A wisp of a woman, she hugged him hard, like a momma bear embracing her cub, even though he had more than a foot on her. Ross hugged her back, inhaling the scents of talcum powder and lilac, scents that he always associated with home.

She dropped her arms and stepped back to survey him. "You look bone-tired, son."

"It's been a long travel day." He looked around her to the two pies set out to cool on the kitchen windowsill. "One of those wouldn't happen to be peach, would it?"

She smiled. "They're both peach and I expect you know that. I was just fixing to put on a pot of coffee. Come on inside."

A while later, Ross sat at the kitchen table across from his mom, a hunk of flaky peach pie and a steaming mug of coffee set in front of him. "Best peach pie in Lamar County," he said, mouth full.

His mother didn't deny it. "I took first prize in the county fair again this year." He followed her gaze to the kitchen wall covered in framed certificates, all bearing blue ribbons.

"Those judges sure are smart." Ross pushed another forkful into his mouth.

Watching him, she shook her head. "You look just like you did when you were sixteen and Amy Johnson turned you down for the sophomore ring dance."

Once, Ross would have found that hard to believe, but being a parent had changed him. Sam might be into Miracle Bras and makeup, but every time he looked at her, he still saw that same sweet toddler fresh off the plane from England.

She stirred her coffee. "I know that look of yours, Ross. It spells girl troubles."

The maternal radar was indeed on point. Appetite gone, Ross put down his fork.

"I'm pretty sure it's not Frannie because you got her out of your system a good long while ago. And I just can't see you with any of those Washington women, either. The only real prospect is that little girl from New York you brought down to help out as your housekeeper. Remind me of her name again."

Ross knew his mother had a mind like a steel trap, but he answered anyway. "MJ. It's short for—"

"Martha Jane," she finished with a smile. "Sweet name, though it doesn't sound much like New York to me."

Ross snorted. "She may not be from New York originally, but believe me, she's a lot more 'New York' than she is anything else. Can't cook for crap," he added, well knowing his mother all but slept in her kitchen. "Turns out all the home-cooked meals she supposedly made us these past weeks came from a personal chef service."

He'd expected his mom to get fired up, but to his surprise she only shrugged. "It's a different day than when you boys were growing up. I'll bet that Rachael Ray hardly ever darkens the door of her own kitchen once she steps out of the studio."

Ross felt his jaw drop. Just when had his old-fashioned mother started sounding like a...*feminist*?

She cocked a brow and leveled him with what over the years he'd come to think of as The Look. "You ever think that maybe, just maybe, it's not so much what's on the table as who's sitting at it across from you?"

He shook his head, not liking how shallow and small-minded he suddenly felt. "I've been down this road before with Frannie. Opposites may attract but they don't stick, not for the long haul."

She let out a heavy sigh. "Land's sakes, Ross, it didn't work out because you two weren't right for each other, not because her piecrust was soggy. Son, if this girl, this MJ, truly touches your heart—and by the woebegone look on your face, I'd bet my last fair ribbon she's wormed her way in good—it seems to me you owe it to yourself and to her to find out why."

As usual, his mom had cut to the core of things. MJ had

touched his heart in ways he hadn't dreamed of, made him feel things he hadn't ever felt for a woman, any woman, before.

"Yes, ma'am, I'll think about it," Ross said. He pushed back his chair, rose, and reached down to clear his dishes as he'd been brought up to do.

For the first time ever, his mother swatted his hand away. "Leave it and go relax. Your daddy will be home soon and Ray's stopping by later. You'd best have a nice restful visit, because it sounds like you have serious business to take care of once you and Samantha get back."

• • •

Standing outside of the *On Top* offices, Macie steeled herself to go inside. Starr was expecting one hell of a story. Considering she was turning up empty-handed after blowing off more than a month's work and thousands of dollars, Macie figured the least she could do was deliver one hell of a show. She took a big breath and pulled open the double glass doors.

"Hi Darcie, happy Monday." Stepping inside, she greeted the receptionist behind the kidney-shaped front station.

"Macie, is it...you?'

"In the flesh." She'd encountered a similar double take moment downstairs at the building security check in.

"Is everyone in the conference room?"

Still looking bemused, the girl nodded. "The staff meeting started a couple of minutes ago. I just dropped off the coffee and bagels."

"Good to know, thanks." She sent Darcie a parting smile and breezed by.

Peering through the clear glass, she saw the meeting was in full swing. Pulling back on the door, she entered. "Hi guys."

Six sets of eyes zeroed in on her, including Terri's and

those of the new Art Director, Matt Landry.

"Nice of you to join us," Starr said from the head of the table. "I gather you're back and prepared to make your presentation?"

"I am," Macie said, slipping into her seat.

A month ago she would have pitched a fit if her skinny soy latte wasn't waiting, but now she reached for one of the unclaimed regular coffees, popped the lid, and dumped in a creamer.

Sipping the weak coffee, she listened with half an ear to the presentation-in-progress, an idea for a new repeating feature, an opinion piece written by a rotation of New York based celebrities that Starr pronounced "very high concept."

Starr turned to Macie. "Next up, we'll hear Macie's report on Operation Cinderella, the Mannon undercover exposé. Macie, take it away."

Macie gathered herself for this, her Big Reveal. Pushing back her chair, she stood. "I was wrong."

"Excuse me?" Starr leaned closer as if she must have misheard. The others followed.

Macie lifted her voice a notch. "I was one hundred percent wrong. I've got nothing on Ross Mannon, and if I couldn't dig up any dirt in more than a month of living under his roof, then it doesn't exist. I'm afraid Operation Cinderella is a bust."

Shocked exclamations made the rounds. Starr's mouth fell open. "What the f — "

"It's true," Macie confirmed, cutting her off. "I realize I built up your expectations, and I'm sorry for that. But not so sorry that I'm willing to sell fiction as fact, to wreck a man's life and his kid's life to sell some magazines. I was wrong about Ross Mannon. I went in sure he must have a mistress or a mister stashed somewhere or at least a really embarrassing kink, but he doesn't." She glanced down at her paper cup and smiled. "If he has a vice, it's that he drinks kind of a lot of coffee."

Starr slammed her fist down on the table, sending the pastry platter and coffee cups jumping. "I send you in for dirt—freaky sex, drug addiction, embezzlement, animal cruelty, something, *anything*—and the best you can come up with is he drinks too much caffeine?"

Macie nodded. "That about sums it up." She'd spent the previous night sleepless and that morning with her stomach churning, but now that she'd dove in, she was actually enjoying herself, not a little but a lot.

Silent until now, Terri spoke up. "I don't understand how you can defend him after everything he said and did. He tried to put us out of business."

Macie focused on her assistant editor, willing her to understand. "Look, we don't have to like his politics, I *don't* like his politics, but I have to say it's pretty hard, almost impossible not to like him. He's every bit as squeaky clean as his public persona. Actually, there is no persona, just an actual person, a person who's honest and honorable, hardworking and kind and a really phenomenal dad."

Starr snorted. "That's all very heartwarming, but how are you proposing to come up with a story, a tell-all exposé, when there's nothing to expose?"

"I'm not. There's no story here, absolutely none."

Her boss tore off her glasses. "Macie, are you…on drugs?"

"No drugs, but you could say I'm high on the truth—and looking around the table I can see there's zero tolerance for the truth here, which is a big reason I'm resigning, effective immediately. My resignation e-mail will land in your inbox by lunchtime."

Starr scowled. "Not so fast. What about the expense monies you burned?"

Macie shrugged. "You can take it out of my final paycheck. If that doesn't cover it, I'll break my 401K. I guess that's all I have. Oh, one more thing. Thanks for the last five years." Her gaze floated back to Terri, whose trembling lower lip made Macie want to cry, too. Determined to hold it together, she went on. "I've learned a lot and I'm going to miss you guys—I'm also going to miss our Fine Wine Fridays and Sushi Saturdays. Those were really great morale boosters even if they were cons to keep us here working after hours, but it's all good. Ciao."

She allowed herself one last look around the conference table of stunned faces and gaping mouths and then she turned and walked out.

The only thing left to do was clear out her office. It was amazing how such a spacious office could contain so very little of her—another framed picture of Stevie, another of her and Pam at the beach a few years back, a Depression Era bud vase she'd found at a flea market, a Container Store plastic bin of random beauty products, including several bottles of nail polish. All in all, packing took under twenty minutes and most of that time was spent staring out the window.

At least I had a great view.

Picking up the full banker's box, she took one last look around and backed out into the hallway—where she collided with Francesca.

The box slipped from her hold, the contents spilling onto the carpet. Macie dropped to her knees to retrieve the scattered articles. So did Francesca.

"I got this," Macie said, deliberately letting her hair fall over her face.

"Don't be absurd. I ran into you." In the midst of picking up the chards of the broken bud vase, Francesca froze. "Bloody hell, I knew I'd met you before!"

Macie opened her mouth to deny it, but what was the point? "I'm the features editor here. Or at least I was until twenty minutes ago."

"They must not pay you terribly well if you have to moonlight as a housekeeper." Glaring, she demanded, "What were you doing in DC at Ross's?"

Now that there was no longer any reason to hide, Macie met her green-eyed gaze head on. "That's really my business."

She started up but Francesca's hand clamped down on her forearm. Gaze narrowing, she said, "I'm warning you, if you do anything, anything at all, to harm Samantha or Ross, you will discover just what a perfect bitch I can be. "

Shrugging her off, Macie picked up the box and stood. "You don't have to worry. You may have trouble believing it right now, and I don't blame you if you do, but I love them both with all my heart."

Francesca followed her to her feet. "Why should I believe a bloody word you say?"

Hugging the box against her, Macie paused to ponder. "Ross and Sam taught me to believe in love again, in fairy tales and Happily Ever Afters. I owe them for that—and so much more."

She shoved the box under her arm and walked away toward reception, leaving Ross's ex staring after her. Reaching the exit, she realized it was true. She did believe in love and fairy tales and Happily Ever After endings again.

Just not for her.

• • •

Resisting the lure of a mega bucks salary increase designed to get him to renew his contract, Ross gave notice that the Friday broadcast would be his last. In lieu of his usual "Ross's

Rant," he used the time to thank not only his sponsors but his listeners.

"I'm not leaving to go on to 'bigger and better things' as some may speculate, but instead to work on becoming one of you all—a better listener. While I'm getting there, I'll be signing off the radio waves and closing down my website, at least for now."

Afterward, feeling strangely at peace, he cleaned out his desk, including getting busy with the paper shredder—talk about catharsis.

"We're gonna miss you around here, Ross."

Engrossed in packing, Ross lifted his head to see the station manager standing in his open office doorway. "Hey, Dale, I didn't see you there, buddy. Come on in." He beckoned the older man inside.

"You sure you won't reconsider?" Dale asked, pulling on one handlebar of his old-fashioned mustache. "I know the bigwigs would love to keep you around."

Ross shook his head. "It's gratifying to be wanted but I've had a good run. Now it's time to get back to the classroom." For the first time, he noticed the rolled-up cylinder tucked beneath Dale's arm.

Following his gaze, Dale unfurled the magazine. Not just any magazine but *the* magazine: *On Top*.

"Oh, yeah, I almost forgot. Legal thought you might want this back. I guess it's just a memento now, huh?" He handed it over.

Reaching out to take it, Ross said, "Yeah, I guess so."

He'd turned the issue over to the legal department on the morning when the blog purporting his porn surfing had broken. Funny, the incident seemed years ago now, rather than just a few weeks.

Dale pushed away from the desk against which he'd

been leaning. "Well, I'd better head home. The traffic out to Fredericksburg isn't getting any thinner with me sitting here. You take care, Ross."

"Thanks. You, too, Dale."

Ross waited for Dale to go. Shredding the magazine wasn't necessary, but it would no doubt feel damned good. He tore off the cover and let the shredder do its thing. Yep, that *did* feel good. He yanked out several pages. The editor's column, "Meet the people who keep *On Top* on top," caught his eye. Curious about who would work there, he skimmed the bios of the key editorial staff. The publicity photo of the features editor, Macie J. Graham, grabbed his attention. Not his type, but still a pretty woman — or at least she would be if she deep-sixed the Goth look and got herself a decent hairstyle, some non-black clothing, and softer makeup. With her porcelain perfect skin, high cheekbones, and lush mouth, she could pass for MJ's evil twin. Heart beating double-time, he held out the magazine, his gaze freezing on the photo. Macie J. Graham. Martha Jane Gray. MJ? A freaky coincidence, it had to be, and yet…

An inner voice told him he'd be a whole lot happier if he just let sleeping dogs lie, but that wasn't who Ross was. It never had been. He *had* to know. He swiveled in his chair and reached for the computer keyboard. Fingers clumsy, he typed the magazine URL into his browser. Within seconds, the home page for *On Top* was loading onto his computer screen, a flourish of red and black lettering with its unmistakable logo. Scrolling down the navigation bar to "Contact Us," he found Macie Graham's direct e-mail address among the listings and typed a quick one-liner. Less than a minute later, her auto-reply landed in his inbox: "I am out of the office on extended leave and unable to reply to your message. If you require immediate assistance, please contact Terri Green at…"

It took every ounce of Ross's self-control to keep from hurtling the laptop across the room. His so-called housekeeper had been playing him for a fool, and he'd been too busy falling in love with her to notice. Worse yet, she'd been out to ruin him. It must have been her who'd leaked Sam's web surfing exploits. Raking hard fingers through his hair, he asked himself what else she could possibly have on him. Before she'd blown into his life, he'd been living like a damned monk, and even in Texas, his sporadic dating had been strictly on the up-and-up.

Yet even now that he'd seen the proof with his own eyes, he found it almost impossible to reconcile the bloodthirsty bitch who'd apparently do anything to get her story with the tender, caring woman who'd made hot chocolate for his kid when she couldn't sleep, soothed him after a hard day with little more than her presence, and treated Sam's Social Studies project as though it were her number one priority on earth.

God, Sam! That must be it, the dirt she'd dug up on him. In helping out with Sam's family tree project, she'd found out about his daughter's illegitimate birth. He didn't give a damn about his own reputation, but he'd hunt her down and wring her neck if she wrote even one word that hurt his baby.

First, though, he'd have to find her.

• • •

Macie was crashed on the couch in her apartment when Franc used his spare key to enter.

She started, surprised to see him. "I thought maybe Terri had forgotten something," she said in response to his raised brows.

Her former assistant editor, now also former friend, had apparently reconciled with her roommate—or so she'd said.

Given how she'd avoided looking Macie in the eye as she'd packed, Macie surmised the speedy decamp had more to do with her persona non grata status than an end to New York real estate woes.

With Stevie sprawled atop her, she went back to watching *The Voice*—with the volume off.

He closed the door behind him and crossed to the coffee table. "Love, you look as though you've been exhumed. Say something."

She dragged her gaze from the TV. "I quit the magazine and I'm leaving New York."

He shoved a fist in the vicinity of his agape mouth. "Dear God, don't say another thing." He dropped down on the cushion beside her. "There's a supposedly fabulous new absinthe bar in the Lower East Side. What do you say we go keep company with the Green Fairy and you can tell Uncle Franc all about it?"

She shook her head. "Thanks, but I hesitate to inflict myself on others right now."

His face fell. "It's the shoes, isn't it? Maddie's legend has turned into a curse. It's all my fault. Well, mine and Nathan's. Actually it's mostly Nathan's—he dragged me to that bloody fundraiser in the first place."

She didn't have the heart to admit she'd re-gifted the red shoes to a fifteen-year-old. Beautiful though they were, they were also inextricably linked with Ross and the Cinderella night they'd shared. She couldn't imagine wearing them with anyone else.

He stood with a sigh. "I'll pour us some wine."

Macie didn't much feel like drinking or having company, but watching him head for her small kitchen, she couldn't seem to summon the energy to object. She'd been dead weight anchored to the couch ever since she'd quit the day before. She heard cabinets being opened, the sound of wine being uncorked, and lastly liquid sloshing into glasses.

Franc returned, carrying two very full glasses of pinot noir. "Inebriate," he ordered, handing her one.

She shifted Stevie to the other cushion, sat up, and took the glass he handed her. "Thanks."

"Okay," he said, settling in beside her, "so basically you're in love with Mannon and in all likelihood he's in love with you but your Dark Secret is keeping you apart, am I right?"

"Yes, that's basically it." He made it sound so simple when it was anything but.

He leaned back against the cushion. "So what are you going to do about it?"

She shrugged. "Nothing."

"Nothing!" He sat up. "You mean you're just going to let him go?"

"Pretty much that's the plan."

"Are you mad?"

Macie set her glass down atop the coffee table. "Crazy mad or crazy in love, it's more or less the same difference."

• • •

Ross may have given up on fairy-tale love for himself, but the last thing he wanted was to pass on his cynicism to Sam. At the same time, he had a duty to prepare her for the worst, including the very real possibility that she would soon see her name in print. During his drive home from the station, he'd racked his brain for the best way to handle things with her, but it wasn't until he pulled into his reserved parking space that the answer hit him.

Tell her the truth.

He wasn't looking forward to letting his daughter in on

what a hypocrite he was, but he also knew it was far better that she hear the truth about her illegitimate birth from him rather than in a magazine or blog.

Moment of truth time, Mannon. Don't blow it.

He knocked on her bedroom door. "We need to have a family meeting, okay?"

"Just the two of us?" She looked beyond him to the hallway, and he didn't have to ask for what—*whom*—she searched.

"Yep, just you and me." Six weeks ago that would have seemed like plenty, but now he couldn't shake the feeling that someone was missing.

Limping into the living room, she asked, "What did I do now?"

In answer, he wrapped his arms around her. "It's not anything you've done, baby. It's what I've done. And it's past time I came clean with you." They sat down on the sofa.

Clearing his throat, he began. "You know your mom and I were seniors in high school when we first met." Ross prided himself on plain speaking, but staring into his daughter's big, wide eyes, tackling the topic of how he'd had premarital sex with her mother suddenly seemed a lot harder than he'd anticipated. His daddy had given him The Talk, a series of halting half sentences and oblique hand gestures that he'd taken in along with his first parentally sanctioned beer. Ray had pitched in, too, gifting him a bootlegged copy of *Debbie Does Dallas*, only the tape was so worn the frames flickered in and out like a relic from the silent film era. He felt a sudden flooding of compassion for his family—and a deep humility for his present ineptitude and past mistakes.

"Dad, it's okay. I know."

Taken aback, he said, "You know... Exactly *what* do you know?"

"I know I was born before you and Mom got married. I've known for a while—and I'm okay with it. I figured you'd get around to telling me someday—when you were ready."

Pulling back, he stared at this amazing creature he'd helped to create and saw that she was a lot more woman than little girl. "You're a pretty smart kid, you know that? Smarter than some adults around here."

They shared a smile. Suddenly Sam sobered. "Daddy… there's something I need to tell you, too."

Just that morning he'd sworn to spend whatever time it took to become a better listener, and it looked like God was fixing to put him to his first test. "Okay, honey, I'm listening."

"It's about why I ran away from New York, why things got so messed up there."

Throat tight, he listened in silence as she explained that a male teacher had been coming on to her. Since staying home from school wasn't an option—not that she hadn't faked a few stomach flus—she'd figured she'd better get out of the city before things got worse.

Thinking of Macie's experience, Ross braced himself. "This teacher, did he touch you or hurt you in any way?"

She shook her head. "It was mostly stuff he said that made me feel weird. He told me I was pretty and one of his smartest students, and yet he kept trying to get me to come to his office after hours for what he called 'extracurricular enrichment,' but I made excuses not to go. Then he gave me a D on an essay test I'm pretty sure should have been at least a B, and all I could think about was I needed to keep up my GPA for college and I got really stressed and angry. It was all so unfair and—"

"You stole the bracelet."

She nodded. "I know it was dumb, and I won't ever do it again, but when Mom grounded me because of the D, I guess

I figured if being good was making bad things happen, maybe I should try being bad and see if it would work the opposite way."

She broke off and Ross wrapped his arm around her even tighter. "I'm real proud of you for telling me. That takes guts. I just wish you'd told your mother or me sooner so we could have fixed things before they got so bad for you." In the spirit of late being better than never, he fully intended to make sure the sick son-of-a-bitch never walked inside another classroom again.

For the time being, he reminded himself to be grateful. Sam had finally let him back into her life where he never should have left. "I haven't been the best of fathers, Sam, I haven't always been there for you when you needed me, but that's going to change starting now. And also, no more secrets. Deal?" He stuck out his hand as he had when she was really little.

Smiling, she grabbed hold. "Deal."

As they shook, he acknowledged he still had more explaining to do, that he needed to break the news that MJ, Macie, wasn't who or what they'd thought. And that she wasn't coming back.

Before he could, the landline rang. Sam grabbed her crutch and popped up to answer it.

"Let it go, honey," Ross called out. "Whoever's calling can leave a message."

Holding her hand over the receiver, Sam shook her head. "It's Mom. Hi, Mom."

Shit, Francesca. Feeling like his brain was fried, Ross shook his head. "Tell her I'll call her back."

Sam held out the cordless for him to take. "She says she needs to talk to you now. She says it's urgent…almost an emergency."

"Samantha, as far as your mother is concerned, just about every damned thing that's happened over the past fifteen years qualifies as almost an emergency."

"Dad, she sounds really upset. She said you'd better get your um...*bum* over to the phone right now."

Rising and snatching away the phone, Ross said, "Francesca, this had better be good. We're in the middle of a pretty major conversation—which I'll fill you in on just as soon as I can—but right now I can't talk."

"Splendid, then for once you can listen."

He scrubbed a hand across his tired eyes. "Okay, what's so all-fired important it can't wait?"

"MJ, *your* MJ, is the Features Editor at *On Top Magazine*. Or at least she was."

"She's not *my* anything, not anymore," Ross snapped, "but yes, I know. Her real name's Macie Graham. I found out a few hours ago. What do you mean by *was*?"

"She gave her resignation this morning."

He hadn't expected that. "I guess after turning in that crack muckraking piece on me, she can just about write her own ticket. Where's she going next, the *New York Times*?"

"Oh, Ross, really, sometimes you can be such a perfect prick. There's no piece on you, muckraking or otherwise, and thanks to Macie there isn't going to be."

That got his attention. "What are you saying?"

"She walked into the morning staff meeting and told her managing editor there was no story, that you were just as wholesome and upfront as your public image, and that she'd wasted both her time and the magazine's money going undercover to investigate a story that doesn't exist. Then she announced her resignation and went to clean out her desk."

MJ had quit her job because of...him? "Why, after working me over for more than a month, would she decide to up and walk away now?"

Francesca let out another of her long sighs. "I'd hoped this might prove to be one of those rare occasions when the blatant truth penetrated your thick Texan skull, but I suppose I shall have to spell it out. She *loves* you, you idiot."

"She loves me?"

"Yes, she does." Ross could hear the smile in Francesca's voice. "Don't you see, Ross? Macie didn't go back to New York to ruin you. She went back to save you."

Ross clicked off the call, feeling as though he'd been sucker punched.

Sam crowded in on him. "What'd she say?"

He hesitated, what was left of the brain housed inside his "thick Texan skull" still working to absorb the news. MJ— Macie—had quit her job, sacrificed her career to save him and Sam from scandal.

"Dad, are you gonna answer or not?"

Meeting his daughter's determined gaze, Ross asked himself the very same question. It was a lot for a kid to take in. Hell, it was a lot for *him* to take in. Before their new open-and-honest policy, he would have tried putting her off, but looking at her now, he could see that wasn't going to work. Macie had touched both of their hearts, not just his. He owed Sam the truth.

"Mom wanted me…*us* to know that MJ quit her job at the New York magazine where she works—*worked*."

Sam let out a whoop. "So when's she coming back? She is coming back, isn't she?"

Ross had thought he couldn't possibly feel any worse, but watching the happiness and hope drain from Sam's eyes, he knew he'd sunk to an all-time low. "No, honey, she's not."

"Have you *asked* her to come back?"

He raked a hand through his hair. "Sam, I can't, not after

she lied to us. She didn't come here just to be our housekeeper. She came here to get a news story on me for her magazine."

"Because you said all that stuff on your show?"

"Well, yes," he admitted, for the first time acknowledging the part he'd played. Had he really imagined he could deliver his Ross's Rant program after program without receiving any retribution? "The point is, even though she did the right thing in the end by killing the story, she still lied to us and that's no basis for a relationship."

"But you and Mom lied to me about being married before I was born. Or at least you didn't tell me on purpose, which is more or less the same thing as a lie, and I'm not going to hold it against you all for the rest of your lives."

Caught, Ross hesitated. "That's...different. It's not the same thing at all."

But Sam wasn't buying. "Is it?" She folded her arms across her chest and stared at him. "You know what I think?"

Not yet, but he'd bet he wouldn't have to wait long.

Her little chin shot straight up, a surefire sign she was signing up for no holds barred battle. Looking him square in the eye, she said, "I think you're a coward."

Having your kid see straight through your bullshit was bad enough. Having her call you on it...well, Ross didn't have a script for that. "Watch it, young lady. You're not too old to be sent to your room, not to mention I can put you on an Internet diet anytime I choose."

But Sam wasn't backing down. As much as she loved Facebook and Twitter and Pinterest and video chatting with her friends, it seemed she loved MJ—Macie—more.

"See, that's what I mean. Any time somebody says something you don't like, you find a way to either shut them up or pack them off."

"Sam, look, I know you're a pretty smart kid—sorry,

young woman—but there's still a lot of stuff about adult relationships you don't fully get yet. And that's okay because you have a lot of years ahead of you to make mistakes and learn from them. But some of us—take me for example—have already racked up plenty of mistakes. From here on, I need to start getting a few things right, okay?"

"But you and MJ love each other, I know you do. I've seen the way you look at her when you think no one's watching. You get all gooey-eyed with that stupid smile."

"Sam, listen up. Sometimes we can love somebody, but that doesn't mean we can live with her."

"You mean like you and Mom?"

He hesitated. "Yes, like me and your mom."

Crossing her arms as though she was the parent and he the kid, she said, "So if I'm hearing you right, what you're saying is that spending the rest of your life with someone you really, really love who really, really loves you back isn't as important as being right about some stupid principle? Well, I know I'm still just a kid, but that sounds pretty wacked to me."

Ross started to answer but stopped himself. "Since you put it that way, I guess it does."

Looking into his daughter's eyes, so clear and incredibly wise, he asked himself if maybe she did have a point. Now that he thought about it, maybe the way he'd led his life up to now, expecting 100 percent perfection from others but falling far short of that himself, was pretty "wacked." Maybe, just maybe, it was time he took a page from the Good Book and started treating others the way he wanted to be treated—with honesty and compassion, forgiveness and yes, love. What better person to start over with than MJ?

"I might be able to get a flight out to New York tonight. Let me call Mrs. Alvarez and see if she can come spend the night."

"Dad! I'm not a baby."

He paused to kiss the top of her head. "You're my baby girl and you always will be."

Ross checked his phone. Fortunately he'd bookmarked several airline websites in his browser. There was a flight to New York leaving out of Reagan National at 7:05 p.m. That gave him just about two hours.

He shook his head. "It's the middle of rush hour. The car would have to have wings to make it to the airport in time. I'd be faster on foot." The latter he said to be facetious, but no doubt about it, DC rush hour traffic was getting uglier all the time.

Sam placed a consoling hand on his shoulder. "Don't worry, Dad. For an old guy, you run pretty fast."

Chapter Eleven

"Let me in, damn it! I want to talk to you. I *need* to talk to you."

Having buzzed Ross into the building, Macie had chickened out at letting him inside the actual apartment. She drew a shaky breath and called through the closed door, "So…talk."

"I need to see you face-to-face. Let me in, *please*."

He didn't ask again. The silence stretched on, broken only by the drumming of her heart. Macie understood that it wasn't only her apartment door Ross was asking her to open to him. It was her heart.

She twisted the deadbolt to the unlocked position and pulled back on the chain. Her damp hand wrapped around the doorknob. She turned it, the brass slipping. The door fell back.

Ross stood in the hallway. Wearing a distressed brown leather jacket and with his shirttail hanging loose, he'd obviously gotten there in a hurry. What looked like an overnight bag was slung over one broad shoulder and in his hand was a big greasy brown bag—the Thai food she'd ordered.

His gaze moved over her, from the towel topping her head to the faux leopard print slippers on her feet. "Interesting outfit."

She folded her arms on her chest, a feeble attempt to hold out against the hurt. "I wasn't expecting...company."

He gestured to the bag of food weighing down his one hand. "The delivery guy showed up after you buzzed me in. I'm more of a pizza man myself, but I'll give Thai a shot. You gonna let me in or do we have to eat dinner out in the hall?"

Face warm, she backed up to let him by.

He walked in, looking around, not that there was much to see: moving boxes, two towers of them; her inflatable mattress; Stevie's litter box and food bowls. Otherwise the place was stripped bare.

"Nice apartment. Décor's a little minimalist for my liking, but then again, you're not exactly the lace doily and flowered curtains type, I guess."

"I guess not."

He carried the food into the kitchen, bypassing the boxes, and Macie followed.

Setting the bag down on the counter and his luggage on the linoleum floor, he turned back to her. "I heard you quit your job. I quit mine, too. I didn't know that meant you were also quitting town."

She opened her mouth to say, "Your ex-wife doesn't waste any time," and then it hit her. "You gave up your show? Why?"

He shrugged. "Being Ross Mannon is no damn fun anymore. I started out studying sociology because I was interested in social relationships, in how people formed groups and then worked to make those groups function. Somehow that got twisted into telling other people what to think, how to behave. I'm tired of hearing myself talk, period. Going forward, I'm going to focus on growing my listening skills and let somebody else do the talking. That goes for my personal life, too." He stepped closer. "Your turn."

Fighting tears, Macie answered, "I'm going home to Indiana to spend some time with my sister and folks and while I'm there, I'll be sending out resumes to environmental groups looking for writers and editors. Working for a nonprofit won't be nearly as high profile or as lucrative as being the features editor of a glitzy publication like *On Top*, but I'm hoping it'll be a lot more meaningful."

Ross still hadn't made a move to touch her, but the look in his eyes was as penetrating as any touch, maybe more so. "It seems we've both been doing a lot of soul-searching." He hesitated, swallowing hard as if gathering his courage, which was crazy because he was probably the bravest person she knew. "Earlier today I had a heart-to-heart with my daughter, who's apparently fifteen going on thirty-five. I'm coming to see that if I'm going to expect complete honesty from others, I'd better start dishing out some myself. Mind if I start with you?"

"O-okay."

"I have a problem I'm hoping you might help me with. I'm crazy in love with you, and I'm not exactly sure what to do about that. Got any ideas?"

Adrenaline pumped through her, enervating her limbs from their lassitude and carrying the seeds of hope. Still, the same obstacles remained. The woman Ross loved might wear her face, but Martha Jane Gray/MJ and Macie Graham were two distinctly different people.

She shook her head. "Oh, Ross, please don't. It'll never

work. We're too different. I'm too…*weird*."

The towel slipped from her head, wet hair spilling onto her shoulders. Reaching out, he lifted a strand and let it slide through his fingers. "I love you, darlin'. I purely love you, and I don't much care whether you want me to call you Martha Jane or Macie or MJ. You can color your hair any shade of the rainbow, wear black every damned day of the week. It won't matter to me because I love you. As for the weird part, according to my daughter I'm 'wacked,' so I guess that makes us just about the perfect couple."

Any other man would have gotten straight to business, peeled off her robe, and made a beeline for the air mattress. But this was Ross—infuriating, old-fashioned, sexy-as-hell Ross. Instead, he took her hands in his. "I missed you."

Tenderness welled and she admitted, "I missed you, too."

He kissed the inside of her wrist then slowly made his way up to the sensitive space inside her elbow. Sensation skittered along the trail his lips made. Inside her slippers, her toes bunched.

She trailed her fingers along the plane of his lean cheek. "You'd better take me to bed before one of us loses her nerve."

Still holding her hand, he looked up. "You feminists are all business, aren't you?" He flashed a smile. "Sorry, Ms. Steinem, but this time we're doing things my way, the old-fashioned way. I want to spend the rest of my life with you. I want us to get married."

After everything, he still wanted to marry her? Shock ripped through her. She tried to hide behind flippancy. "Why, are you pregnant?"

He grimaced. "Don't be cute. When a man asks you to marry him, there are only two answers: yes or no. And, by the way, I'm not taking any no's."

She ran a hand through her tangled wet hair. She was

a mess, inside and out. "But Ross, I don't cook. I barely microwave."

"Good thing. I was starting to put on weight."

"And I'm a lousy housekeeper, a serious slob."

"I'll hire a cleaning service. I hear you can get a good one for cheap."

"Ross, I don't know. I'm not sure we—"

"Stop, take a breath, and answer me one thing." He paused. "Do you love me?"

Her throat felt so thick, it might have been packed with peanut butter. "You know I do."

"And I love you, which pretty much synchs it."

He bent to unzip his carry-on. Fishing inside, he brought out a box—the shoebox holding her red slippers. Lifting off the lid, he reached inside and took out one of the shoes. "I had it fixed." Kneeling, he beckoned for her to give him her foot. Macie hesitated and then stretched out her leg. "We can go to Tiffany's tomorrow and pick out the ring together, but for now maybe this can seal the deal." He slipped off the leopard print bootie and replaced it with the vintage shoe.

Looking up at her, he melted her with his gaze. "You have to admit Macie Mannon has a hell of a nice ring to it."

Flexing her slipper-shod foot, Macie shook her head. He was absolutely infuriating, absolutely perfect for her. She was sure they had years of sparring ahead of them. She could hardly wait to start.

"Make that Macie *Graham*-Mannon, and you've got yourself a deal."

"So much for matching monogrammed towels." He shook his head but his eyes twinkled like the crystals studding her red shoes. "I can see life with you isn't about to get boring anytime soon."

It was Macie's turn to smile. "You've got that right,

Professor. In fact, you might as well know upfront I plan to keep you on your toes for the rest of our lives."

Standing, he took hold of her shoulders and pulled her close. "Good, because I seriously love you. And there's only one thing I'm gonna ask from you once we're married."

Warmth splashed her cheek. Damn, she was crying. Smiling anyway, she answered, "Great sex?"

He grinned. "Well, on second thought, make it two things." His eyes turned serious. "Don't you ever stop loving me, got it?"

Macie nodded. "Got it. Are you going to at least kiss me now?"

He slid his hand into her still damp hair and drew her closer. "Yes, ma'am, I am."

His mouth met hers. Soulful and sweet, passionate and patient, the kiss was different from any other they'd shared so far, a pact against holding onto the past, a promise of all the happiness yet to come.

Pulling back, she searched his face. "Is Sam okay with this? I mean, our getting married will affect her a lot. I feel like we should at least talk to her first."

"Who do you think got me to put aside my pride and come here? That kid is almost as crazy about you as her old man is."

"That settles it, Prince Charming." Heart overflowing, she added, "I want the gold ring, the keys to the kingdom, the whole enchilada of the fairy tale." She flexed her foot again. Was it her imagination or did her toes...tingle? "And the shoes, can't forget them."

His megawatt smile was bright enough to light up all the billboards of Times Square. "Call me old-fashioned, but I'm hoping there's a Happily-Ever-After in there somewhere."

Taking his face between her palms, Macie smiled. The

past was the past, but fairy tales were all about the future.

"Definitely, Ross. Happily Ever After—you can count on it."

Epilogue

ETERNITY—AKA THE GREAT BEYOND

"Brava, well played, Macie!" Silver-screen legend Maddie Mulligan pulled her gaze from the portal to Earth and clapped her satin-gloved hands. "Carlos, my love, we must celebrate! Bring the bubbly."

"Champers it is," he called, pouring from the perennial bottle of pink champagne on ice. Attired in an ascot and velvet smoking jacket, his dark hair combed back with Brylcreem, he crossed the dressing room carrying two champagne flutes. Handing one to Maddie, he lifted his in a toast. "You were splendid, my darling. Cecil B. DeMille could not have done a better job of directing."

They touched glasses, setting off a soft tinkling. Or perhaps the tinkling was a bell signaling yet another angel had received his or her wings. It was hard to tell. The Great Beyond was a bustling place; acoustics could be a problem. So could the frequent fallout of feathers. Angels were perfectly lovely beings, but they had an unfortunate tendency to molt.

"It was the shoes, darling," Maddie said, glancing

downward to her slipper-shod feet. Like the other features of her studio dressing room, the red velvet heels were an exact divine replica of the ones she'd had on earth. "I just helped get them into the proper hands—and onto the proper feet." She took another sip of champagne. "But we mustn't be smug, my darling. Our work is but beginning."

They exchanged looks. In unison, they said, "The friends!"

Reaching up to adjust her stole, she said, "There's Francesca, so chic and lovely on the outside and yet so sad and lonely on the inside."

"And we mustn't forget Stefanie," Carlos put in.

Maddie nodded. "The poor child's been living as a Cinderella indeed, and now that horrible stepmother and those stick thin stepsisters have her believing she's fat rather than voluptuous. Convincing her to see herself as desirable will take some doing, but I've no doubt the shoes will once again prove equal to the task."

"What of poor little Cynthia?" Carlos asked.

Maddie paused. "Poor little…*Cynthia*?"

"Cynthia Starling, Starr. The managing editor of that dreadful periodical," he clarified.

With her red curls, light blue eyes, and pale freckle-dusted skin, Starr looked to be at least partly Irish. Given her blocked-off heart and curmudgeon ways, she also promised to be the most difficult of the remaining three. A daughter of Erin herself, even if she had long ago lost her lilt, Maddie had a soft spot for a fellow countrywoman.

She smiled. "Christmas is coming up. If there was ever a time to bring a fairy tale to fruition, it's the winter holidays."

Carlos toasted again. "To Starr, Francesca, and Stefanie, I can hardly wait to see how their stories will unfold."

Maddie sent him a warm smile. "It won't always be easy," she admitted, reaching out to flick a feather from his lapel.

"Each has her unique gifts and strengths, but also faces her unique challenges. Still, I feel hopeful their stories will end, or rather begin, as ours has."

On cue, the strains of a waltz sounded. Their champagne glasses disappeared. Carlos bowed and, straightening, offered his arm to his wife. Dimpling, she took it. Spinning them out onto the studio soundstage, he whispered, "Happily Ever After doesn't get any better than this, does it?"

Smiling, Maddie lifted her lips to his. "No, my darling, it most assuredly does not."

Acknowledgments

To my family and friends for their unflappable love, humor, and support, notably my partner, Raj Moorjani, and my friend and fellow author, Mary Rodgers; to my wonderful literary agent, Louise Fury, for her steadfast advocacy, positivity, and friendship; and to my editor, Stacy Cantor Abrams, and the talented Entangled team for being such a delight to work with throughout the publication process.

About the Author

Award-winning author Hope Tarr earned a Master's Degree in Psychology and a PhD in Education before facing the hard truth: she wasn't interested in analyzing people or teaching them. What she really wanted was to write about them! To date, Hope has written twenty historical and contemporary romance novels for multiple publishers including *Operation Cinderella*, the launch of her Suddenly Cinderella contemporary series for Entangled Publishing. Hope is also a co-founder and current principal of Lady Jane's Salon™, New York City's first and only monthly romance reading series, now in its fourth year with satellite salons nationwide. Look for additional Suddenly Cinderella books starting with Starr's story in *A Cinderella Christmas Carol* (November 2012) and find Hope online at her websites at www.HopeTarr.com and www.LadyJaneSalonNYC.com as well as on Twitter (@ HopeTarr) and Facebook (www.Facebook.com/HopeC.Tarr).

17019970R00136

Made in the USA
Charleston, SC
22 January 2013